The Novels of Mary

The
Patten
Experiment

The Larks Press

First printed and published in England by
T. Fisher Unwin, London, ?1899

New edition published in September 2006 by
The Larks Press
Ordnance Farmhouse, Guist Bottom, Dereham,
Norfolk NR20 5PF
01328 829207

Printed by the Lanceni Press, Garrood Drive, Fakenham,
Norfolk. 01328 851578

British Library Cataloguing-in-Publication-Data
A catalogue record for this book is available from the British Library

A full catalogue of Larks Press books is available on
www.booksatlarkspress.co.uk

Foreword

by Ronald Blythe

Farming was in crisis when Mary Mann wrote this, to us, somewhat strange novel. There was what the *Eastern Daily Press* called, in its worried editorials, 'the flight from the land' as great numbers of half-starved labourers and their families fled their tied cottages for the cities. Mary Mann's neighbour, Sir Henry Rider Haggard, had been commissioned by the government to examine a predicament which was affecting the whole country. His conclusions appeared in a wonderful book called *Rural England* (1902). A text from the Bible was on the title page: 'The highways were unoccupied...the inhabitants of the villages ceased.' The farmers themselves called it 'the coming down time'. Profits were non-existent and wages were a pittance. Where he and Mary Mann and her husband farmed in the Waveney Valley the latter were eleven shillings a week, the hours almost endless and the hardship terrible. Both writers did all they could to reveal the plight of the labourer, Rider Haggard in *A Farmer's Year*, his commonplace book for 1898, and of course Mary Mann in her tough and realistic stories.

The Patten Experiment would have been sensational in its day. The young people up at the Hall are idealistic, so they decide to live on a labourer's wages in a tied cottage for a week, just to see what the poor had to put up with. Eustace Patten, a curate newly married to Rica Boyan, his brother Tony, and Rosamund, Bel and Bay Boyan of Bunwick Hall are the chief Experimenters. The two small girls have to go to school alongside the dirty youngsters from all around. The class differences add to their economic difficulties. They are squeezed between a bad neighbour and a fairly reasonable neighbour at Cherry Tree Cottages. The workhouse is just up the road.

At first the experiment is fun. It is a novelty to light stick fires in the grate, fetch drinking water from the well, and show Bel and Bay how to play without toys. But hunger and exhaustion set in in no time at all. Dealing first hand with the dreadful Mrs Nobbs on one side and the moderately nice Mrs Chaney on the other, not to mention an appalling rector's wife, Mrs Dodman, who hands out anti-drink tracts and tells Rosamund to put her long hair up, is at first amusing, and then a horror.

Food is the greatest challenge. They have been accustomed to eating well; now a piece of pork must last for days. Eustace, the curate, goes turnip-hoeing with the labourers in the hot sun and becomes ill. His

3

handsome brother goes to the pub, learns to snare Mr Boyan's rabbits and is about to be tried by the bench when, after all kinds of misadventures, they return to Bunwick Hall and civilisation.

What Mary Mann does best is to show the unbridgeable gap between the rural classes, not only in speech – she is unmatched when it comes to Norfolk dialect – but in physique. The work-stunted poor are set against the beauty of her hero Tony who will, the reader fears, die on the Western Front. He seems to be the only one among the Experimenters with common sense. All the rest of them go to pieces in various ways as the week proceeds. A kind of 'east is east and west is west', classwise, prevails. Ultimately there is no meeting point for the farm labourers and the gentry of Dulditch. Due to Rider Haggard's *Rural England* we know that both are victims of the agricultural depression. But Mary Mann reveals, in what would have been a quite revolutionary manner at the time, village people crippled by their 'position' in life. No wonder there was that famous flight from the land. Her sympathies would have made her contemporaries uncomfortable.

Wormingford, 2006

4

CHAPTER ONE

How They came to Make it

'MANY a time,' said Mrs Boyan, 'I have tried to plan out their money for my own satisfaction; so much for grocery, so much for bread, rent, clothes; and I have failed to discover how they keep fairly healthy, fairly shod, fairly covered on, say, eleven shillings a week.'

'But you, my dear woman,' her husband said, 'have spent four-and-twenty years of your life in attempting to prove that a thing which is done around you with perfect ease and simplicity from year's end to year's end can't be done at all.'

The Boyans were sitting with their family over their own luxurious breakfast table, and were discussing, with that mild persistency on the one side and that hardly-restrained exasperation on the other which characterised all their debates, the condition of the agricultural labourer.

'Your mother,' Mr Boyan continued, turning to his children, 'is a little mad on this subject. Don't pay any attention to her, please. She demoralises the people by a pity which is quite uncalled for, and impoverishes me by charities for which she gets no thanks.'

'Thanks!' echoed Mrs Boyan, faintly, closing her eyes and leaning back in her chair. She re-opened them upon her young people presently. 'Their thankfulness makes me ashamed,' she said.

'Alas! the gratitude of men
Hath often left me mourning,'

quoted Tony Patten, who had come in late for breakfast, and knew nothing of the argument.

'The people are far better off than we are,' Mr Boyan went on. 'My men have no cares, no responsibilities. Every fortnight as payday comes round they receive a fortnight's wage; whether they've earned it or no they get it, whether I can afford it or no I pay them.'

'Extremely liberal of you!' the wife of his bosom ejaculated, mildly ironical.

'Do they care that the land left me by my father, and to him by his father, and so on and so on, for half a dozen generations, is worth about a third now of its original market value? Have they to study appearances, as we have to do, or as you, woman-like, think we have to do? Have they a son to send to college, and daughters' – here he stopped for a moment in his loudly-voiced interrogations, and made a grimace at Rica, the eldest girl, sitting by her husband's side – 'to marry?'

'As if you had anything to do with my marriage! I married myself, daddy,' said Rica, who is rather proud of that achievement at present.

'Shut up, darling!' her husband said. He was the Rev. Eustace Patten, and with his eye-glasses turning from one to the other, he was listening with attention to the conversation.

'When,' went on the father of the family, resuming his theme with its appropriate note of irritation, 'when I have to sell my wheat at a price at which I can't possibly grow it, when I can't sell my bullocks at all, when the lambs are dying by scores in the wet spring, and the pigs have swine fever, is there one of my men who lies awake for a quarter of an hour's uneasiness?'

'But you forget it is not all misfortune,' Mrs Boyan reminded him. 'When the flocks prosper it is your gain, not the shepherd's. When you sell a pair of home-bred horses for a couple of hundred guineas, as you did last week, when you get a double crop of corn, you have some joyful moments of prosperity. Then, we may have some anxieties about Christmas bills, and Dolly's college expenses, but we don't have to send our children hungry to bed, and we haven't to look forward to the workhouse as the only provision for our old age.'

At this Mr Boyan, in the exasperation of his spirits, hit the table with a flat hand, making the tea cups and saucers to ring, and pushed his chair back – he always permitted himself such outward and visible signs of anger, in order that there might be no mistake about its being the genuine article – and appealed to the Reverend Eustace, qualified by two months' experience of matrimony, to sympathise with him on the surpassing stupidity of woman.

'Yes, but –' said Eustace.

He paused there, looking earnestly at Mr Boyan through his glasses, his always sufficiently accentuated jaw stuck forward, and a little to one side, and wearing that air of wishing entirely to master his subject before he gave an opinion upon it, which was found so trying by the frivolous-minded young Boyans. 'The question is,' he went on presently, '*is* eleven shillings a-week enough for a man to live on, work on, bring up his family on? Mind!' lifting up a restraining hand as he saw his father-in-law about to sputter forth a reply, 'I'm not saying it isn't – I'm not wishing to argue – I'm trying to get at the root of the thing.'

<hr>

'He wants reliable information, daddy, not heated invective,' Rica explained, taking her husband under protection with the little superior air of the matron.

6

'– Is it possible for a man, and say – well – five children –'

'Eight,' supplied Mrs Boyan. 'One of our labourers has eight children, Eustace.'

Eustace stuck out his jaw at Mrs Boyan and shook his head. 'We won't be extreme,' he said. 'We'll say six – six children to live on a labourer's wage?'

'My dear fellow, don't ask me,' Mr Boyan said, smiling largely, with an air of open candour. 'Don't ask me, ask them, the men themselves. Don't they do it? I've nineteen men, not counting the steward, employed on the home farm. At Dulditch, which I have the felicity of farming myself since poor Robinson smashed up, there are another dozen men. Is each one of that nineteen and that dozen men –'

'Thirty-one, sir,' supplied Tony. 'Simple addition.'

' – performing a miracle, do you think, every day he reports himself alive and well and ready to work? His children keep up the attendance at school –'

'Even when they are in an obviously unsound state of health,' insinuated Mrs Boyan. 'We have had measles amongst the children this year, we have had whooping-cough, influenza, chicken-pox, and a peculiarly disagreeable skin disease.'

'Well, what can you expect of such a rotten set?' demanded Mr Boyan. But, before that injudicious remark could be pounced on by his listeners – 'And don't other people's children have illnesses?' he shouted, in the tone to which Mrs Boyan always replied by silence, and by down-dropped, quivering lids.

Her husband, having achieved the desired result, turned in tamer mood to Eustace. 'The fact is,' he explained, 'my wife puts all sorts of pernicious notions into these people's heads. She's a good woman; would go hungry herself, if need be, to give to others to eat, but she can't understand' – here he looked at the lady at the other end of the table, smiling her little superior smile with eyes still closed, and struck the table smartly again with his open hand and raised his voice – 'she *can't* understand the mischief she makes and the dissatisfaction she's the cause of.'

'I see,' said Eustace, gravely accepting the statement. He nodded his head once or twice at his father-in-law, and then turned his eye-glasses upon Mrs Boyan as if he were considering her for the first time, 'I should like, however, to know –' he began, and there stopped, jaw on one side, meditating.

'You know much more than is good for you, old man, already,' Tony, his brother, assured him. And breakfast being over, Rica dragged her husband into the garden; and for all the happy hours of that summer day, the subject, which had inexpressibly bored the younger members of the family in the early hours of the morning, was forgotten.

However, as it chanced, before the shades of night fell, it obtruded itself again.

Some of the young people, indefatigable in obtaining for themselves all of air and sunshine and exercise they could, had been for a bicycling ride since dinner, and returning from that expedition, sat out to enjoy the cool of the evening upon and about the wide white steps of the stone-pillared porch, which adorned the principal entrance to Bunwick Hall. The Reverend Eustace Patten had fetched from indoors a cushion for his wife to sit on, and she had spread forth the skirt of her dress for his accommodation. In the west the rosy tints of evening had died away, while over some Scotch firs to the left of the house, and behind which the pointed roofs of riding-stables and coach-house were visible, a young moon sailed up, soft and silvery, into the blue.

Upon the hard gravel sweep before the porch sat Tony Patten, embracing his knees drawn up to his chin, and on either side of him, close to him as they could conveniently sit, and adopting his attitude, were Bel and Bay, the youngest of the Boyan family. They sat so close and kept so still because long ago they had said good-night to father and mother, because, now and then, across the stillness of the evening, came to their ears the voice of the maid whose duty it was to see them to bed calling from the garden at the back of the house where she ineffectually sought them. 'Miss Bay! Miss Bel!' called poor Maria. Between the elder of these children and Rosamond, the brown-faced, brown-haired girl, who sat in the centre of the centre step, and in pauses of the desultory conversation peremptorily ordered her sisters to go to bed, was an interval of ten years.

Mary, in point of age between Rosamond and Rica, pale faced, calm eyed, a young edition of her handsome mother, sat upon the flat-topped pedestal which finished the stone balustrade flanking the wide doorsteps and gazed upon the moon.

'It's the first time I've seen it,' she said.

Whereupon Bel remarked that it was lucky she had not seen it through glass, then, for that Maria – Maria's voice had sounded farther away the last she called, and Bel had found courage to speak – had caught sight of the last new moon through the schoolroom window, and her young man had gone out walking with another young woman the very next Sunday afternoon!

'Turn your money and wish,' advised Rosamond, sharply. But Mary had no money, not even a purse. Tony Patten put down one leg, and jingling some loose coin in his trousers pocket, held out a sixpence on his palm to her. So the girl, slipping from her pedestal, went to him, and turning the money in his hand, bowed three times gravely to the moon. They saw her lips move as she told the desire of her heart to the goddess of the night, burdened with how many secrets already!

'I know what Mary's wish was as well as if she'd spoken it aloud,' Rosamond announced; and Mary blushed swiftly at that speech. It was not at her, however, that Rosamond looked with the searching, restless gaze of her seventeen years, but at the young man, now hugging his knees again on the gravel.

'Perhaps you know what was mine also?' Tony inquired of her.

'If it is what I think it is, it won't come true, and so I tell you,' the girl declared with some eagerness.

'But, you see, you know nothing about it; and I mean that it shall come true,' Tony asserted.

He was a rather handsome young man, long-limbed, clean-looking, athletic, with not a superfluous ounce of flesh on all his well-made carcase, and not a superfluous penny in his pocket. He had not long left college, and was relying more on his Blue than his degree for his future advancement. Not quite the sort of young man to encourage about a house full of marriageable daughters, as Mr and Mrs Boyan were apt to remind each other with asperity, when one or the other – as one or the other was sure to do – asked Tony down for his holidays.

'It can't be right,' suddenly said Eustace, pursuing aloud a train of thought, which had hitherto kept him silent, 'that a large section of society should be compelled to live on an income insufficient to provide the bare necessaries of life. On the other hand, your father can't afford to pay more, he says; and if he could afford it, the tenant farmers certainly couldn't. Eleven shillings a week! How is it possibly done, Rica? You and I think we shall be in a tight enough place with a living bringing us in two hundred and fifty.'

(The Reverend Eustace Patten had recently been appointed to the living of West Wackham, in a neighbouring county, but was not yet inducted.)

Rica, striving with all her little brain to become a practical member of society, inquired how much, at two hundred and fifty a year, would be coming in per week; and hearing that it would be considerably over four pounds ten, and knowing that people lived on eleven shillings, she heaved a contented sigh, squeezed closer to her husband's side, and remarked that she thought they would be very rich indeed.

'Yes, but – never mind us – how does a man and his family live on eleven shillings a week, love?'

'Love' had not considered that question. 'They do it,' she said. It seemed to her an unanswerable argument. She rubbed her cheek against Eustace's shoulder, and shut her eyes. She and he were so happy, need they think about other people's worrying affairs?

'Yes, but,' persisted the clergyman, 'oughtn't we to know? We're going to live with the agricultural labourer, remember, probably for the rest of our lives – you and I.'

'I give you six months of him before you change livings with someone in the slums of somewhere; or before you go off as chaplain to the Bishop of a fever-haunted swamp in Africa,' Tony said, breaking off a soft serenade he had been whistling to the young moon to make that prophecy.

Rica lifted her cheek to whisper an anxious question in her husband's ear.

'No, darling; of course not,' he reassured her; and with a contemptuous glance at the disturbing Tony, she nestled into position again.

'It's no joke to be the wife of the Reverend Eustace Patten,' Tony remarked to the little girls beside him.

He had to bend his head to catch the eager whisper of the elder. 'We'd rather be your wives, Tony; Mary and Rosamond would too. We all often say so.'

'If you nearly quite shut your eyes,' said Rosamond, each of whose own eyes at that moment was nothing but a sparkle between black lashes, 'and look at those peaked roofs of the stable and the coach-house among the trees, you can almost fancy they are mountain-tops, with that sweet little bit of a moon shining down on them.'

'Name two mountains in the county of Norfolk,' Tony commanded the children at his shoulders, who, taken unawares, promptly mentioned Snowdon and Vesuvius, and were much applauded.

'When father and mother are dead, and Dolly brings his horrid, *horrid* wife to live here, I shall betake myself to a country where there are mountains,' Rosamond announced, still gazing through nearly-closed lids at the peaks of the only range within view. 'Then I shall half-shut my eyes like this, and they will, I daresay, remind me of the stable and coach-house at home, and I shall wish I were back with you all, sitting on the door-steps.'

'My dear child, you're not gone yet!' Mary reminded her.

'We'll certainly drop a tear when the time comes,' Tony promised. 'I know what Eustace is driving at,' he went on, 'only he's afraid to break it to Rica, poor fellow. He wants to leave the lap of luxury and his wife's apron-strings to go to starve in a labourer's family for a week or so to see how he likes it.'

Rica raised an angry head, and gazed with eyes that had a little fright in them at her brother-in-law. 'He wants nothing of the kind,' she answered fiercely. 'You want nothing of the kind, do you, darling?' she inquired in another tone of her husband, who muttered a perfervid word of reassurance. 'Of course,' announced Rica, for the benefit of the assembly, 'if Eustace did wish to do it, I should do it too.' Her usually mild blue eyes glared round upon the group. In those first days of her married life, gentle and unsuspicious little girl as she was by nature, she looked upon the rest of the world as so many enemies engaged in a ceaseless plotting to tear her from the arms of her Eustace.

'If you wish to do it, I will do it too,' she assured him.

'Let's all do it,' Mary Boyan suggested in the placid way so like her mother's. 'Let's see what it's like to live huddled together in a house that covers about ten yards of land. Let's see if it's so agreeable as daddy says to go about our work with half-nourished bodies. I agree with Eustace; we ought to know. Let's try it.'

CHAPTER TWO

They Prepare for the Fun

IT was so that the Boyan family came to make the experiment which caused a good deal of comment in the neighbourhood, and of which some of them repented after.

'Anyone can put up with anything for a week,' Tony said. And they all assured each other that it would be amusing, if nothing else, and that no possible harm could come out of it.

'No harm, and possibly good,' Mrs Boyan thoughtfully admitted.

Mr Boyan put himself in opposition; in that woman-ridden household, as he had confidentially explained to his son-in-law, he was compelled habitually to adopt that attitude in order to maintain any semblance of the balance of power. It was not a very effective policy, as he may or may not have been aware, and it is a melancholy fact that the accustomed phrase, 'I won't allow it,' made very little difference in the family arrangements. He had declared no daughter of his should ever ride a bicycle, should ever appear in private theatricals, should ever become a nurse, should marry a man with a less income than five hundred a year. But Rica's husband, with only half that fortune, had carried off the prettiest, most petted of all the pretty, petted children. Mary was to start on her training at Guy's in a week's time; Mr Boyan had laughed louder than anyone at the farce of '*A Pair of Lunatics*' as acted by Tony Patten and Rosamond in the village schoolroom at Easter, and he had himself presented each of his grown-up girls with bicycles on their several birthdays last year.

Therefore, although his family were too well brought up openly to defy their father, they made preparations for the Experiment all the same.

It was decided by Mrs Boyan that it should not be attempted in their own parish, where the proceedings would arouse an interest likely to prove embarrassing among their neighbours of all classes, but in the adjoining village of Dulditch, where was the Brightlands farm, unlet, and therefore temporarily under the management of the bailiff. The Boyans were well-known in Dulditch, of course, but not so intimately as in the home parish.

Now, there happened to be in Dulditch a cottage, the centre one of a row of three standing by themselves on a meadow removed from the village, which was in the hire of a certain old servant of the Boyan family, at the present moment away from home nursing an invalid sister. Eustace and Tony cycled over and inspected this dwelling, pronounced it 'a frightfully healthy and jolly-looking little place,' with a tiny garden, gay with flowers; the green grass of the wide, sloping meadow, running up to the little front gate.

This cottage, then, for the consideration of a shilling for the week's rent, Nurse Brunton was glad to place at the convenience of her old master's family.

'That will leave us just ten shillings a week,' Eustace explained, thoughtfully. He had by this time gone fully into the question, and he informed the others of the party, that at least a further eighteenpence must be put by for clubs. The Oddfellows' Club, in case he happened to be ill and required a doctor, the Burial Club, lest it should come to pass that he or Rica died, the Boot Club and the Clothing Club, into which,

12

he was assured, all the provident among the labouring class managed to pay. There was also to be deducted from the capital in hand the weekly shilling which the bread-winner of the family kept back for his private expenses, beer and tobacco.

'Which leaves us exactly seven shillings and sixpence – you see, for food, firing, light,' Eustace said, a little doubtfully, looking at Rica with his jaw wrung aside. 'A fraction less than one and a penny a day.'

Rica thought they would find it enough. Of course it was enough, or how did all the people manage? And Bel and Bay – Bel and the Dragon as they were facetiously called in the family – jumped for joy when they were told they would not be expected to eat meat. For a whole week they pictured themselves rioting on a diet of 'farthing sponges' (a comestible to the elder taste of a peculiarly sawdusty and flavourless composition), washed down with copious draughts of champagne cider, biscuit and beverage to be bought at the Bunwick village shop, and upon which all the stray pennies finding their way to the pockets of the lesser Boyans were expended.

Mrs Boyan had been at first reluctant to let the two children share in the hardships of the experiment; but when Eustace sensibly pointed out to her it was quite impossible to discover how a man and his wife and children could live on so much money if there were no children, the good lady saw the reasonableness of the statement, and, not without misgiving, withdrew her objection. Bel and the Dragon ran wild with delight at the prospect before them. They chased each other for a whole day up and down stairs, round the garden, across the meadow, and screamed excitedly when caught. Their heavy brown hair flew about the brims of their muslin hats, their sturdy legs and their dark eyes danced with joy and jollity. They were a pretty pair, and on whatever subject the elder Boyans disagreed, they agreed in adoring and petting the 'little ones.'

It had been at first arranged that Eustace, Rica and the children should form the party in Nurse Brunton's cottage in Cherry-tree Row; but Eustace had soon bethought him that, while he was away labouring in the fields, and while Bel and the Dragon were at school (he had insisted on their being sent for the week to the Board School –'they will probably learn more there than they will learn with Rosamond in six months,' he declared, and added that there was no good in making the trial unless they went in for the whole thing thoroughly), Rica would be lonely in the cottage. It was suggested, then, that Mary, who was not due at Guy's for ten days yet, should join the little family as another child. Either of the children ate as much as she. She could take the place of the big girl, just through the fifth standard, who was kept away from school to help 'mother.'

'Which means,' said Tony to Rosamond, 'that Mary will do the work of the place while Rica moons about after her husband.'

'You let Mary fight her own battles!' said Rosamond, quickly. 'She has got all the champions she wants. In season and out of season it is always "Mary, Mary, Mary," with you. Mary is all very well, but Mary continually – !'

'And if Mary's to be the eldest child, where do I come in?' Tony asked of Mrs Boyan.

'You?' enquired Mary's mother, with a little unusual crispness of tone. 'You will stay where you are, and help Rosamond and me to get on without the others.'

'I think not,' Tony said. 'I don't propose to myself to feast in idleness here while my only brother earns his bread by the sweat of his brow, and the ladies of my acquaintance perish with hunger. What becomes of the young unmarried men, who work for Mr Boyan, and have no homes of their own?'

'The hobbledehoys,' explained Rosamond.

'They lodge with the families,' Mrs Boyan told him.

'Then I will be a hobbledehoy, and lodge with Rica,' Tony decided.

It was after she learnt of this addition to the volunteers that Mrs Boyan withdrew Mary. Mary had so little time to be with her parents, and, the others being all away, it would be so agreeable for her father and mother to go with Mary to London, and to see her settled in her new quarters before they returned. A couple of trustworthy servants could be left in the house, the rest going for a holiday, and so on, with many minute domestic details. If any one was wanted to bear Rica company, let it be Rosamond.

'There's always Rosamond to fill a gap,' that young lady remarked. It amused her sometimes to pose as the 'put-upon' one of the family. She permitted herself, by way of diversion, to be jealous of her sister Mary, and in idle moments hugged the theory that 'nobody cared for Rosamond.'

It was arranged that the new tenants of the Cherry-tree Cottage should migrate there on the Saturday afternoon, take the Sunday to settle down in, and to accommodate themselves to their surroundings, and begin life fair and square on Monday morning.

In the meantime the weather was very warm, and the Boyans, loving ₁, lived out of doors. Also, being extremely fond of each other, ent about as a rule in a single company, the principal topic of

14

conversation among them at that time being how their week's money was to be laid out to the best advantage. They were none of them fools; even Rica, before the advent of Eustace, had been given to insist on her possession of brains, although she had lost interest in the matter of late. When one had such a clever husband, what did it matter? But the rest, having opinions of their own, were apt to assert them with unnecessary vehemence. Calling in lumps of white chalk and cedar pencil to their assistance, they in this instance asserted them, with detrimental effect, on any convenient surface offering itself to their calculations as they moved about through the idle, summer days.

Chalked on the brown paint of the coach-house door, some hieroglyphics are still visible, which once legibly set forth such a reckoning as that which follows:—

	S.	D.
Bread, ...	1	0
Candles,...	0	6
Cheese,...	0	6
Breakfast bacon, ...	2	0
Tea, ...	1	0
Sugar, ...	0	8
Coal, ...	1	6
Flour, ...	1	6

'There does not appear to be anything left for meat,' Eustace said when he had added up that sum.

'Besides, it comes to eight and eightpence, and we've only got seven and six,' Rosamond derisively pointed out. She had not approved the expenditure for breakfast bacon, and had thought the two shillings might be more advantageously laid out in potted bloaters and jam.

Mrs Boyan, who had happened to see the above computation, criticised it with severity.

'Are you aware, my dear Eustace,' she enquired, 'that you must allow half a stone of bread or flour for each of you, children as well as yourselves? Your allowance for bread is ridiculous.'

So Eustace groaned, and flung away the chalk.

Then someone remembered that if Tony was a lodger he must pay for his lodging, and it was found that six shillings a week was the usual charge.

'For that, Rica must do my washing and my mending; and, you mayn't have noticed it, but my appetite is good,' Tony reminded them.

So, when it was found that, instead of the seven and sixpence a week left to them after the deduction of rent, club money and Eustace's pocket money, thirteen and sixpence would be at their disposal, they took heart of grace, and coming to a halt against the white-painted dairy shutter, Eustace drew forth a piece of lead pencil, with which, and with a higher courage, they once more made calculation.

	S.	D.
Three stones of flour at 1/6,...	4	6
Oil and candles,...	0	6
Coal,...	0	6
Grocery,...	2	0
Butcher's meat,...		

Eustace was of opinion that, with bone and waste reckoned in, they must allow a pound for each person a day. This, in the seven days, amounted to twenty-one pounds of meat. Twenty-one pounds at even sixpence a pound was – well, it was quite impracticable. Eustace made up his mouth for a silent whistle, restored his pencil to his waistcoat pocket, and temporarily turned his back on the subject.

It was Rica who first grew tired of detail, and stipulated that there should be no more calculation.

'There is so much in environment,' Rica pointed out, sagely. 'People who are fitted into a place always know how to fill it. Once settled in the cottage, we shall lead the cottager's life by intuition, Eustace.'

So they stopped bothering their heads over the problem of making two ends meet, and gave themselves up to the prospective enjoyment of the fun in store for them.

'I don't believe you will find it quite so funny as any of you expect,' Mrs Boyan said.

CHAPTER THREE

They Make a Beginning

SO, when the Saturday afternoon came, each one carrying in a bundle under his arm the few necessaries which, in his new position, would be d, the little company found themselves deposited at the door of tre cottage in Cherry-tree Row, Dulditch.

Before leaving home, Eustace and his brother had emptied their pockets conscientiously of all moneys but the twenty-two shillings which had been paid them beforehand for their week's wage – a precaution uncalled for in the case of the young Boyans, who were never known to have money in their pockets by any chance.

'If we haven't the money, we can't spend it,' Eustace pointed out.

'I shall chum up to Tony,' Rosamond declared. 'When you've paid your six shillings for your board and lodging, you've got five more left in your purse, and nothing to squander it on, Tony.'

Tony regarded her thoughtfully. 'Being unmarried,' he reminded her, 'and with a natural desire to make myself agreeable in the eyes of the fair sex, it is only reasonable that I pay more attention to my outer man than such a family man as poor old Eustace, for instance. There will be expenditure for such trifles as hair oil' – here Bel set up a shout of derision – 'a green or a blue bow to wear around my collar of a Sunday' – here he was compelled to pause to beat off the savage attacks of Bay, who objected to neckties in these colours – 'there are, besides, the clubs to keep up. Then, again, I think of getting married some day. I should like to lay aside at least three shillings a week towards provision for my future home. Also, being young and light-hearted, I likes my glass and my pipe, Rosamond; I shall have to stand a pint to a friend or two. A bachelor can't be mean –'

'And there's Bay and me will like to go to the shop with you sometimes,' Bel reminded him.

Nurse Brunton was a flower-lover. While the little patch of garden before the house on either hand was weed-grown and neglected, hers was well stocked, well tended, a tiny spot of sweetness and colour. Big plants of pale and dark blue delphinium were there, the tall flower spikes as high as the cottage door. There were yellow marigolds, cheerfully self-assertive, great bushy mallows, with their myriad blooms of rose and white; round the window a monthly rose was trained; by the tiny gate was a tall sunflower or two, not yet in bloom. Sweet-scented stocks and asters, purple and white, loved of the poor, filled up the spaces left by the larger growths.

The windows of both the downstairs rooms were choked with plants, watered with tea and soap-suds, protected from sun and frost by sheets of newspaper introduced between them and the glass. Geraniums, fuchsias, petunias, striped mauve and white, flourished, to the exceeding pride of Mrs Brunton, and also to the effectual excluding of sunlight from her rooms.

'What nice plants!'

The Experimentalists stood at last in the front room of the cottage which was, for the time, to be to them as home, and it was Rica who broke the silence which had fallen upon them by that remark. 'I think we will put some of them outside to get the benefit of the air. Please leave the door wide open, Eustace. But they are very nice.'

Truth to tell, the front room, with its cramped space, its airlessness, its stuffy smell, was a little damping to the spirits of the party. Mrs Brunton was a well-to-do woman in her way, and all the possessions dear to the soul of the cottager were hers, and crowded within the four walls of the best room. There were the six red-coloured, highly-varnished deal chairs standing on the border of red brick outside the square of bright-coloured carpet; there was the chest of drawers and the round centre table of the same evil-smelling material. Upon these reposed, each upon his mat, and at regulated interval from his neighbour, butter-dish, Bible, glass decanter, a gay-coloured tin which had once held biscuits, a pair of china dogs, with blue bows about their necks, and various specimens of the glass ornament which John Pedlar brings round, with cheap laces and pins and combed-out orange and magenta mats, to charm the treasured savings of the year from the pockets of the labourers' wives. On the drab-coloured walls, papered, as the crinkly set of the paper showed, by the thrifty hands of Nurse Brunton herself, were hung pictures of a scriptural theme, calculated to make an artistic person extremely wicked; some mourning cards in frames of gold; a nurseryman's coloured advertisement abomination.

Upon these splendours the eyes of the newcomers fell a little blankly; they looked at each other with glances of misgiving, but even the youngest of them knew she must not begin with complaint.

'I wonder what is the first thing to be done?' Rica demanded of her husband.

'Perhaps you'd better light the fire for tea, dear,' he suggested. 'We shall all feel more at home when we've had a cup of tea.'

Rica moved her eyes from her husband's face to the shining little stove. She went towards it with a reluctant step and a little vagueness of mien. For worlds she would not at that moment admit she did not know how to light a fire.

'Let's have a look at our bedrooms first,' Rosamond suggested.

So up the steep, hollow-sounding little stairway they all trudged, Eustace, solemn of face, his cap pushed to the back of his head, leading the way, Bel and the Dragon stumping, with small outbursts of giggling, behind.

In all Mr Boyan's cottages are three bedrooms; in each room, tiny as it is, a fireplace. 'Where's the good of trying to teach decent care for their health and morality to people that herd together like pigs in a sty?' he had said when, years ago, he had inherited his little estate and the old disgraceful cottages had been pulled down and the new built. But the landlord did not find that the labourers and their wives were anxious to avail themselves of the better condition. They preferred, indeed, as residences the old clay-built, thatched cottages on the next farm, where all the ground space was occupied by the fair-sized kitchen, and where, in one 'chamber,' under the rat-riddled roof, father, mother and children could lie sociably together.

It is true that of these desirable dwellings the rent was ten shillings a year less than that of the Cherry-tree Cottages – a quite sufficient difference to account for their popularity.

Bel danced with delight when she saw the little box of a room apportioned to the lodger. 'Tony's legs will certainly dangle out of bed!' she cried with interest.

'Even then I must set the door open to make room for them,' Tony reflected.

'For goodness' sake, Tony, keep your boots on, or it won't be lespectable,' Bay cautioned him.

She and Bel were highly gratified at the prospect of sleeping, one at the head and one at the foot, in Rosamond's bed, and at once began to wrangle about who should be that happy one who first had the privilege of the foot. They jumped together excitedly hand in hand, delighted at the amount of noise to be got out of the bare boards. They promised each other with glee that they would not go to sleep at all, but that Rosamond should tell them tales the whole night long.

The boards were scrupulously clean, the linen looked fresh and white. Rica set the windows open hastily, to remove that familiar smell of the close sleeping-room with which even the clothes of the poor are impregnated. There was no breeze, but the warm air was soft and sweet with the scent of the flowers in the garden below; a wide expanse of meadow, whose closely-nibbled grass was beginning to scorch in the long-prevailing drought, rolled in a gentle slope to the road, not visible between its hedges. Beyond the road the land rose gently again. A big ash tree grew at the left-hand corner of the Cherry-tree gardens. 'It is there that in the pauses of labour I will smoke my pipe and meditate on "the good which the benignant law of Heaven has hung about me,"' Tony said to himself, looking out of the tiny window.

Bringing in his head, he remarked that he would thank them all to keep their beds of a morning until his ablutions at the pump were performed. He called on them to observe that his room was quite artlessly innocent of all toilette requisites.

In truth, the arrangements in this respect were altogether Arcadian. That was as it should be, Eustace maintained. For a week they were to live in Arcady.

One advantage arising from the inspection of the sleeping apartments was, that the living-rooms, by comparison, appeared more satisfactory. Indeed, the family had not lived for twenty-four hours in Cherry-tree Cottages before they came to regard their front room with something like awe. From the first they decided that its splendours must not be familiarly treated – one had only to look at the varnish on the chairs to see at once they had never been sat upon. The newcomers, therefore, followed the custom of the country, and took up their abode in the kitchen.

It was there that they presently lit their first fire. Rosamond and Tony lit it, they having discovered a small stack of sticks stored in the outhouse. Being lit, and the kettle beginning comfortably to murmur, one of them suddenly remembered that there was no tea.

'No tea! And, of course! why, we have nothing,' Rica cried.

'You're responsible for that. You are housekeeper,' Rosamond reminded her. And Rica, casting appealing glances around, took down the basket from its peg behind the door, and went forth to do her shopping.

'Eustace had better go with her to take care of her,' Rosamond advised, but Tony declared that his brother must stop at home to chop the sticks. 'We've got to keep this thing boiling till she comes back,' he said, gently indicating the kettle with the toe of his boot; whereupon, the sticks beneath suddenly collapsing, the kettle turned on its side and put out the fire with its contents.

By the time Rica had returned the fire had been lit and relit many times, and Rosamond, very hot and cross, was black in face and hands. Eustace was but an indifferent woodman; in spite of unsparing exertion only very small chips of wood came in.

'Of course we must have some coal,' Tony said angrily at last. 'The coal should have been stocked before we came here.'

At this Bel and Bay, who had been rushing around on a tour of inspection, announced that they knew where there was quite a large heap of coal.

'Then, idiots, go at once and fetch it,' the irritated fire-makers commanded.

It was quite useless to scold them because they brought it in their clean white pinafores; for, as they eagerly pointed out, what else was there for them to bring in? But Rosamond scolded all the same, and Tony, who was always on the side of the pretty and the oppressed, scolded back, and quite a hubbub was going on when Rica returned. The kitchen did not look clean any longer, for the children, startled by Rosamond's outcry, had shot their load of coal on to the red bricks just inside the door, and bits of stick and ash had been carried by the spilt water and deposited in hollows in different parts of the uneven floor. But, at least, the fire was blazing brightly, and the kettle sending forth volumes of steam.

Rica was very hot and tired. She had tried to run home, but the basket was so heavy, her hand and arm still shook with its weight. Her purchases had come to a great deal of money, too, and she was so anxious and dispirited that Eustace insisted she should not be bothered to lay the table. Surely it would not hurt Rosamond to lay the table alone!

Nothing would hurt Rosamond, that young woman declared. She, in the eyes of the Pattens, at least, was of no account. Rica was an angel, and Mary a Solomon – only Rosamond was as the dirt beneath their feet.

This, while she flung on the tablecloth, rattled the cups and saucers into their places, threw the tea into the teapot.

'For Heaven's sake, play light with the tea!' the others cried. 'It's got to last a week, remember!'

'She's put in a good quarter-of-a-pound,' Tony declared.

'Scrape it out again, please!' Rica cried in tones of wild anxiety.

And it was scraped out; but tea from the village shop, at one and four the pound, was found to be not of the best, and before any flavour could be got into the brew, every leaf was returned to the pot, to the triumph of the persecuted Rosamond.

Good temper and good spirits were, however, restored by the time the little party sat down to their first meal at the round table of the sunny kitchen. The fire had made the small space unbearably hot, and window and door were set wide open. Through the latter could be seen the oblong space of gravelled yard common to the three cottages. In its midst the drab-painted pump. Beyond was the strip of garden ground for the growth of vegetables and fruit. The kitchen boasted only four full-sized chairs, but a small wooden chair, painted green, with a railed back, and a three-legged stool to match, the property of Nurse Brunton's son, now fighting the Dervishes 'neath Egyptian skies, were appropriated by the children, who sat to take their meal outside the door, their cups upon their knees. Whenever they laughed their knees joggled; and whenever their knees joggled their tea was spilt, Bay explained hilariously, coming in for the fourth time to have their cups replenished.

It had been explained to them that they might take either butter to their bread or marmalade, but they must, on no account, have both together. After a whispered consultation, Bay's little dimpled face flattening Bel's pretty nose, by way of showing that they were very confidential, they decided to have butter first and then marmalade.

No objection could be taken to that plan, and it was one that the others also pursued; but it was a little alarming, at the end of the repast, to find that a whole jar of marmalade, costing fivepence halfpenny, was finished, and a loaf and a half of bread was eaten.

'We can't reckon the cost of the meal at less than tenpence,' Eustace said. 'How many meals shall we want in seven days, Rica? and how many tenpences go in thirteen and six?'

The result, when worked out, was nothing less than disconcerting.

'It is evident that in some way we have been extravagant,' Eustace said, pushing out his reflective jaw at his wife.

Tony opened eyes of alarm at his brother.

'I vow I can't support nature on less than I've had to-night,' he said.

'The worst is, when we do labourer's work we shall probably be even hungrier,' Eustace reflected dismally.

'And the breadwinners mustn't be hungry,' Rica eagerly declared.

Later, she took the opportunity to impart to Rosamond her view of the situation. 'You and I mustn't eat so much,' she said. 'The men want it, and the children want it. We are only women. We've heard of the self-sacrifice of the poor. This is where it begins, Rosamond.'

It was while she was expounding this grand idea that their ears were startled by an angry voice hailing some nameless person from the little outhouses where the fuel was stored. No reply was made but the smothered laughter of the two little girls huddling together against the door. Soon the same voice was heard shrilly repeating a question, –

'Who've took my coal? Who've been a-meddlin' with what didn't consarn 'em, and a-takin' of my coal?'

'We took some coal,' Bel's little clear voice made answer. 'We took it to make our fire.'

Upon which the Boyans' left-hand neighbour, Mrs Nobbs, advanced from the outhouse, and looked in at their open door. She was not the most agreeable among the labourers' wives, as they soon discovered to their cost.

'Play-actin' is play-actin',' she asserted oracularly; 'but howsoever that be, I'll thank you to leave my coal alone.'

'We had to light our fire and we naturally took the coal,' Rosamond said, looking haughtily upon the intruder.

'We will pay you, of course,' Rica said.

She was quite pale – never before had she been spoken to in such a tone. Through all her youth she had nourished a secret fear of the village policeman. She almost felt his hand upon her shoulder now.

'At how much do you value the coals we have used?' Rosamond demanded sternly, and Mrs Nobbs, with the eyes of greed, surveyed the fireplace and the stray pieces of coal scattered over the floor. 'Coals was hard enough for such as her to come by,' she said, sullenly apologetic. 'She couldn't consider herself paid with a farden under sixpence.

Having received that sum without a word of acknowledgement, she fetched from her own house brush and dust-pan, and returning, collected the bits of coal besprinkling the floor, muttering as she did so, and evidently still considering herself very ill-used.

'Bang goes sixpence!' said Rosamond, when once more her back was turned. 'We won't steal any more of Mrs Nobbs's things, Rica. It's too expensive.'

CHAPTER FOUR

Frightfully Jolly

IT was while the girls were washing up the tea-cups on the first evening that they made the acquaintance of their right-hand neighbour, Mrs Chaney. She was a well-featured, pleasant-faced, middle-aged woman, clean and neat in appearance, offering a welcome contrast in every particular to the good lady on the other side.

'I heard my neighbour a-bawlin' at you, ma'am and miss,' she said, 'and I've dropped in to give you the hint as you mustn't take no notice. She've sech a won'erful quare temper have Mrs Nobbs. She's likelies to put herself out right onpleasant, give her the chanst.'

'What is she like when she's more unpleasant than she is now?' Rosamond inquired.

'She've got such a nasty ways, Mrs Nobbs have; there ain't no accountin' for her, as I say times and agin to my husban'. She poured a kittle of bilin' water over as butiful a row o' young peas o' mine as ivver you see in your life last Tuesday fortnight, and for no other rayson but that her Dan flung a stone and nigh cut my Horus's eye out.'

'What a perfectly awful woman!'

'Yes, miss. She's won'erful contrairy, as I say to my husban'. She broke the pie-dish as I lent her 'cause she han't one of her own t'other day, and she's that wild she han't spoke a word to me since. I knowed what was up, 'cause I found the pieces hulled in at my front door.'

This good woman was very useful in showing the sisters where Nurse Brunton kept the few household articles needful for her simple management, in helping them to tidy up the kitchen, and in giving them what counsel and advice she thought needful.

'Mrs Chaney,' Rica said, 'do tell us how you make the money go round. We thought it so easy – you all do it, and so we thought it must be easy. But things seem very expensive. Just look at the few little miserable things Mrs Barrett gave me for two-and-sevenpence-ha'penny, Mrs Chaney.'

So Mrs Chaney sniffed at the cheese, weighed the pound of butter in her fingers, appraised the other contents of Rica's basket.

'Of course, miss,' she said, 'you've got your ma to fall back on.' But Rica explained that this was by no means the case.

'Look here,' Rosamond said, 'if we *die of starvation*, we've got to live on eleven shillings a week, and you've got to tell us how to do it. Now, how much a meal do you reckon to allow each person?'

Mrs Chaney shook her head. 'If you're goin' to parcel it out so,' she said, 'you'll never do it. Try to plan the money and you'll go downright crazy a-findin' out it can't be done. There ain't no rules, and there can't be. Sometimes you go without this, and sometimes without that. Sometimes you pinch tight here, and sometimes 'tis there. Times you get into debt when you can't help yourself, till the day comes round when you don't want so much coal, nor yet no candles, and then you pay up –'

'Debt,' said Rosamond, pausing in the process of wiping the Britannia-metal teaspoons, and with a sudden lighting of her face. 'Ah! that helps, I expect.'

'I don't recommend it,' said Mrs Chaney, dispassionately. 'I've a dread on't myself, but times you're drove to it.'

24

'And about meat, Mrs Chaney? Can you manage meat for one meal a day?'

'I bake a bit of pork, Sat'days – most weeks. We ate the gravy hot, wi' dumplins and p'taties, Sat'days; and the whole on us get a slice, cold, o' the Sundays. Cold go the fuddest. 'Tis only a manager such as Mrs Nobbs that cut here j'int up hot.'

'And when do you bake again?'

'I reckon to eke it out till th' Thursday, and then mayhap I get a slice o' bacon to fry for my man – a man must have his taste o' meat, I say.'

'And you and the children?'

'We haven't the work to do,' said Mrs Chaney, simply.

'But you must live!'

'Well, 'tis jest how 't happen. Times there's an apple dumplin'. I bile down the guseberries and currans in the garden into jam – the children are won'erful fond o' jam with their bread. Truth is, I can't tell no one how we manage, miss; I don't know myself. It seem to come, thank the Lord!'

Tony was smoking his pipe over the little gate which opened upon the meadow. A dozen cart-horses had been turned out for their weekly holiday. They were galloping heavily round the meadow, their great hoofs striking the ground with hollow thuds, little clouds of dried grass and of powdery soil flying from beneath their trampling feet. Here and there, one rolling ungainly on his broad back kept the Sabbath after his own contented fashion.

'This is really frightfully jolly,' Tony said to Rosamond, who had joined him there. He waved his pipe to include the peaceful landscape and the evening sky. 'I believe your father's right after all, and a farm labourer's life is one free from care and of great blessings. To live in a splendid solitude, intimate only with the "mute, inanimate things" of nature. To have no thought of what the morrow may bring forth, no regrets for an untempted, sinless past –'

'To have no past, no future, no place among the reasoning sons of men,' Rosamond continued. 'To work from week end to week end with eyes on the furrows, and never, never on the skies, and only not to starve –'

'Oh, come!' said Tony, 'one would think you were your own mother, Rosamond.'

'I've got cares enough on my shoulders to be the mother of all of you. I am not particularly anxious about you, you are splendidly strong, and I'm strong too; we shall stand it. But it is pretty clear to me that Eustace and Rica and the little ones will be reduced to the last stage of weakness in about three days on the diet which is prescribed.'

'Come to that, we can pitch it up,' said Tony, contentedly smoking his pipe.

Rosamond flung him a scornful look. 'As if you did not know your own brother better than that,' she said. 'The worse things got, the deadlier Eustace would stick. He'd think it a feather in the cap of his noble resolution to see his wife and the little ones reduced to a state of emaciation. He'd die cheerfully himself for the pleasure of having had his own narrow-minded way.'

'Gently! Eustace isn't narrow-minded, my good girl. He's an enthusiast, I admit – a faddist, if you like.'

'And a faddist is a dangerous person, and should never be entrusted with wife and children. I always say he shouldn't be allowed to marry Rica; that he was much too cracked.'

'Look here, shut up!' said Tony. 'You aren't of an age to have any opinions.'

'I'm of an age to express them,' Rosamond said.

She was turning away then, but he stayed her for an instant with a hand upon her arm.

'We mustn't let Rica and the children take any harm, you know.'

'I don't intend that they shall,' said Rosamond, with her chin in the air.

She found Eustace and her sister at the end of the long narrow plot of ground at the back of the cottage. A tall hedge of scarlet-runners divided this little strip, filled mostly with potato and onion beds, from the field at the back, and the clergyman was gathering the scarlet beans while his wife held the basket. He was gathering under difficulties, having only one hand to spare, the other being round his wife's waist, while her head was rubbing against his shoulder.

'Rica is a little disheartened already,' he explained to Rosamond. 'I tell her it's the first step which costs; once in the stream you – eh?'

'Swim like a duck,' supplied Rosamond, 'or perhaps a goose. We'll say a goose. My own opinion is, we shall find the whole thing as easy as easy. I have been turning things over in my own mind, and I can see that we shall manage extremely well.'

Eustace looked at his young sister-in-law, immensely relieved. She was only seventeen, and her bronze-brown hair still flew free over her red-brown cheek, and fell heavily, unfettered, down her back; her face, freckled over its short, straight nose, and beneath the dark, bright, unresting eyes, still retained a sort of baby roundness and plumpness. But there was character, for all that, in the prettily-cut, full lips, in the carriage of the head, in the movement of the shapely brown hands, even.

She was young, certainly, but she was a person on whom to rely, Eustace felt in that moment, not having thought much about the girl before.

'Having begun a thing, we must, of course, go through with it,' he said.

'Of course,' the girl assented. 'You'd have to be a quite superior person to venture to say that there was no necessity. All the same, it isn't part of the undertaking that Rica, who was always the delicate one among us, should tire herself any more with walking to the shop, and there are one or two things she has forgotten. If you'll find the little ones, Rica, and put them to bed, I'll go and fetch the bit o' pork for to-morrow's dinner. Hand over the purse.'

'There seems so little in it,' Rica said anxiously.

'It'll serve. You didn't get enough bread, but there's quite a supply of butter still, and you forgot the candles, and the oil for the lamp, and the salt, and the pepper, and the vinegar, and the soap, but there's a whole pound of rice – only puddings won't be very nice without milk, I'm afraid – and we shall live like fighting cocks.'

'Perhaps, as it is so far for you to fetch the things, you'd better let Rosamond keep the purse and do the shopping, darling,' Eustace suggested. Rica was glad to retire from the responsibility, and that was the very arrangement Rosamond desired.

She pulled her garden hat down from its peg behind the front door, where all their outdoor garments hung, and emptying the beans from the only basket the establishment boasted, and swinging it about her head in youthful exaltation of spirit, she ran down the narrow garden path and out of the gate, which Tony pushed open for her. He closed the gate with a little bang after her, and she stopped and turned in her passage across the meadow as she heard it.

'I say,' she called, and beckoned him with the basket swung high.

'Say on,' he shouted, 'I've no secrets.'

But she beckoned him with the basket still, and he, albeit with misgiving, walked slowly up to her.

'It's a secret. I want to whisper,' she said.

So he bent his head to hers.

'Don't you wish it was *Mary* instead of me?' she asked him. 'Wouldn't it be pleasant to walk beside her to Mrs Barrett's and to help to carry the basket home?'

He made no answer to that question, but sauntered back to the gate again, smoking his pipe.

'Mary wouldn't have him, even if he'd money enough to marry her,' Rosamond said to herself as she walked on. 'And I think it a beastly shame' – she was often a little forcible in her manner of expressing herself – 'that, until he asks her and she refuses him, he should be allowed to go on wasting all sorts of rubbishing fancies on her. If ever,' went on the girl, flinging up her basket and catching it by the handle – a work requiring some address – 'anyone gets so foolish over me, and I don't feel a bit "gone," I shall tell him so straight out and put him out of his misery. Why shouldn't a girl be straight in her love affairs as well as in other things?' She paused a minute over the reflection that a certain course she had it in her mind to pursue was not a particularly direct one. 'But Eustace is such a fool,' she finished.

Although she was only Rosamond and not Mary, she found Tony waiting to help her carry the basket home.

'I've bought the barest necessaries,' she said. 'You couldn't buy more at Mrs Barrett's with your heart's blood, because she hasn't got it; and we've only bread enough to take us over till Monday; and, look, there's just three and sixpence left in the purse.'

CHAPTER FIVE

Plain Living and High Thinking

'LABOURERS' wives never go to church on the Sunday morning,' Rica pointed out.

'Labourers' wives should,' said the clergyman. 'You see, my dear Rica, we're not here only to prove to our own satisfaction that this thing can be done, we're here also to show to the agricultural poor *how* it should be done. We won't begin by setting a bad example. Besides, surely one woman is enough to cook one piece of pork; and there is Rosamond.'

Rica considerately offered to leave the little ones behind to help with the cooking. 'Take them, for Heaven's sake! and keep them out of mischief,' Rosamond cried.

For, truth to tell, the children, under the straitened conditions, and in the restricted space, were a nuisance and nothing else. They missed their dolls and toys. There was little use in pointing out to them that cottage children had no toys, and that they must amuse themselves without them. They wanted experience in the art of being happy in this new mode of existence, and only hung about complainingly, hindering the older girls in their work.

A speech of Rica's, to the effect that a girl of Bel's age next door had to carry her baby-sister about from morning till night, inspired the elder child with the fatal ambition to become the dragon's nurse. For Tony's admiration, leaning upon the garden gate, she gathered the fat little sister in her arms, staggered with her to the hardest part of the meadow roadway, where, becoming suddenly weak from laughter, she dropped her and straightway fell on the top. But for the fear that the young man, who was the children's hero, should look upon her with contemptuous eyes, Bay's grief over her broken, painful knees would have been loud and long. But when Tony was there to wipe the wounds with his beautiful large pocket handkerchief, you naturally tried your best not to scream; and when he threw you up on his shoulder and galloped over the grass with you just like a horse, it joggled your sobs into laughing somehow, and you were all right.

<hr>

It was when the rest of the family was gone to church and the kitchen cleared for operations, that Rosamond's troubles began. Then it was found that two fires must be kept going, for the pork had to be baked in the little oven in the wall, and the potatoes and beans to be boiled on the kitchen fire. The coals were lent by Mrs Chaney on this occasion, and Rosamond gave that kind woman the munificent order to lay her in a half hundred on the morrow. She was exceedingly surprised, when these were duly stocked in the outhouse, to see how small was the supply.

'Did you think a half hundred was a ton?' she was sarcastically asked.

'It sounds *much* more than a ton,' she said loftily.

Rosamond was only an indifferent stoker. 'When you've got to consider each little bit of coal you put on the fire it's awful,' she said, with a heated face. But that Tony presently came to her assistance the task would never have been accomplished.

They had had water porridge and bread for their breakfast, and the young man found the smell of the roasting meat appetising.

'I tell you what,' he said. 'I don't call this the coolest or cleanest or pleasantest occupation for a hot Sunday morning, and you're the biggest duffer I ever saw at the work, Rosamond, but I rather think I shall punish the pork when we fall to.'

'You imagine, perhaps, that you are going to eat the pork hot?' Rosamond inquired. 'You and Eustace, with appetites like pigs, and all of us? I am sorry to disappoint you. The j'int is simply to smell of to-day – to smell of, and to grease the potatoes with; of which fattening vegetable you will observe I am cooking a large allowance.'

'You mean we're not going to taste meat to-day again?' Tony inquired, lifting a scorched and threatening face from the meat he was basting. 'You mean that?'

There was something so menacing in his aspect, and in the determined way he handled the spoon he was using, that Rosamond found it wise to reassure him. She laughed at the fierceness of his face.

'A man is capable of doing murder for the sake of his "little bit o' pork,"' she said disdainfully. 'I should be ashamed to be the slave of my own passions if I were a man, Tony.'

'And, being a girl, you should be ashamed to talk about what you don't understand,' retorted Tony; but he returned to his labours with the spoon.

'Well, then, you're going to have your meat, sure enough, to-day. We're all going to have it. They don't have it in the other labourers' cottages, you understand, but you need not tell Eustace that. You and I have good consciences, Tony, but it is by means of a little winking.'

'I don't mind winking in a good cause,' Tony admitted.

'We do better than our neighbours because I'm such a good manager, you understand.'

'You'll be a treasure to some young man on eleven shillings a week when you grow up,' Tony reflected.

'Me? Rosamond? It's Mary that's the treasure. (Oh, Tony, that's the second time! *Don't* let your tobacco-ash into the baking-pan. However hungry we are it will taste.) It's always being impressed on me the treasure that Mary is.'

'By me?'

'There! Of course some salt should have been boiled with the potatoes! Why couldn't you remind me, Tony?'

'By me?'

'Don't repeat questions in that superior tone. It's horribly irritating. What does it matter by whom? It is nothing to you. By that poor little weedy-looking curate of ours among others.'

30

'And does Mary – ?'

'Why, of course she does! Do you keep your eyes shut that you can't see what's before your nose? And daddy won't let her, and quite right of daddy. If ever I want to be such a fool – which I sha'n't – I hope daddy won't let me! So my lady's going away to be a nurse, and when she's about thirty and worn to a thread, perhaps he'll have got a living and can marry her. Set of idiots!'

'I'm not going to fight the curate's battles, but your sister Mary isn't an idiot, let me tell you. Wherever she goes, and whoever she marries, she is one of the sweetest girls I have ever seen in my life; mind that!'

'So she is,' said Rosamond. 'All the same, I get a little *sick* of my "sister Mary." I say! That's a little *too* much! The pipe turned abso-lute-ly round in your mouth and the whole of its contents fell out on the pork that time.'

'Oh, bless the pork!' said Tony, walking off.

'The grace is a little "previous," but the meat won't be the worse, I am sure,' said Rosamond.

He stood silently for a while in the cottage doorway, gazing down the sunlit strip of kitchen garden to the wall of scarlet-runners at the end. But, after a few minutes, Rosamond missed him from that position, and peeping through the screen of geraniums and petunias in the window, discovered the young man a few yards from her, his hands in the pockets of his white flannel trousers, looking with an appearance of absorbed interest at the pump.

Rosamond considered him in silence for a minute, and in her face might be read a mingling of interest, of impatience, and of ruth.

'Let's hope it will spoil his appetite,' she said, setting her teeth. 'If only he can't eat his dinner, what a good morning's work I shall have done!'

Beneath the window, planted among the stones, was a little border of violet-hued stocks. The scent of them rose up to Rosamond's heated face, peering between the geranium leaves; the murmur of the 'dim-eyed, curious bee,' busy among the cloying sweets, floated on the still air. Some swallows, who, year after year, returned to their undisturbed nests beneath the cottage roof, darted out and wheeled high in the sunshine. One of the three old hens which Mrs Chaney kept in the woodshed across the way, laying an egg at this juncture, commented loudly and insistently on the fact. And Tony stood in the oblong gravel-yard, seemingly oblivious of all about him, and stared upon the pump.

Rosamond flung out to him with a pail of zinc, glittering bright. 'Since you can't tear yourself away from the pump you may as well turn the attraction to some account and get some water,' she told him.

When he returned with the full pail to the kitchen she was mixing together flour and baking-powder and water in a basin. She stirred the paste with the vigour which, rightly or wrongly applied, characterised all her actions; and as she bent above her work, the end of a heavy brown lock of hair which fell across her cheek dipped in the basin.

'These are dumplings,' she explained with pride. 'Mrs Chaney told me how to make them. You eat them with the pork, Tony, to make the meat hold out.'

Tony contemplated the mess with a dissatisfied air. 'Talk of tobacco in gravy! I call hair in dumpling a hundred times more disgusting,' he announced.

'Yes, I thought you'd had your dinner,' retorted Rosamond. 'You took it with some rue at the pump.'

The spoon flew round with added energy, some still unmixed flour sprinkled itself wildly in all directions, and again the tiresome lock fell forward and dipped in the basin.

'A single hair in the food is enough to destroy the heartiest appetite,' Tony pursued, 'but a whole wig like that of yours in the dish –'

'If you think I'm going to spoil the dumplings for the sake of a hair or two you are much mistaken,' said Rosamond, loftily. Then, hastily descending from her eminence, as her manner was, 'Here, tie my hair up then if you like,' she said. 'My hands are all messy and I haven't got the time.'

So, while she completed the dumplings, rolling them into little balls on a board, he stood behind her and wove the heavy loose hair into braids.

'There's three of them,' he informed her. 'You look like a horse going to a fair.'

'I didn't ask you what I looked like. Pin them up. Haven't you any hairpins? Alan Mason, who came down from Christ Church with Dolly at Easter, made a collection of hairpins while he was with us. He picked them up when Mary and Rica dropped them, and kept them in his cigarette case. They said it was frightfully useful. They always knew where to go.'

'I have one hairpin. I use it for my pipe. I wouldn't give it to you to save your head – hardly. But I've a cedar pencil at your service if that's any good.'

And they found a small bundle of wooden skewers in the drawer where the knives and forks were kept; so that, in spite of cries of pain, stampings of the foot and wild scoldings from Rosamond, he managed at length to fasten the braids about her head.

'The effect mayn't be handsome, but I'll warrant your hair don't come down,' he said.

'Gracious, heavenly powers! What a sight!' the others exclaimed when they came home from church.

It was Tony and Rosamond who, having cooked the dinner, dished it up.

When the little party sat round the table, their eyes, filled with a hungry interest, fastened themselves upon the loin of pork which, in the tin where it had been baked, graced the centre of the cloth, the largest dish not having been found big enough to hold the joint. In a yellow basin lined with white smoked the beans. There being no other receptacle for the potatoes, it was found convenient to help them straight from the saucepan placed on the fender. Eustace looked on this manœuvre with the eyes of favour.

'To have things served hot is half the battle,' he said.

The family gazed rather shyly upon a steaming, white-looking mass which took its place opposite the principal viand.

'These are dumplings,' Rosamond explained with natural pride. 'Eaten with the pork, they blunt the edge of the appetite.'

It appeared likely that they would do so, and they all accepted them dutifully. But only Eustace and their proud creator made much way with them, the former not so much from appetite as a stern sense of duty.

'If not so extremely sloppy they would appear to be very wholesome and satisfying – certainly satisfying,' he said.

'You see, if we've got to live on eleven shillings a week we can't afford to be dainty,' Rosamond pointed out, advancing the indisputable statement in irritable tones.

'Exactly so,' Eustace agreed. He laid down his knife and fork and looked round upon the plates through the eyeglasses which never left his nose. 'There must be no waste,' he admonished. 'Courage, Bel and Bay. Rica, my dear one' – Rica was turning over the contents of her plate and looking very white – 'I think I can manage your portion and mine too, love. Another slice of the meat for Rica, Tony, to make up for the loss of the – the dumpling.'

At the close of the one and only course it was discovered that the eyes of Bay, the fat and petted, were full of tears – tears which had welled up there at the thought of a certain Sunday pudding which always graced the middle-day Sabbath dinner at Bunwick Hall, and to which Bay Boyan was particularly partial. As a diversion, she and Bel were allowed to help their eldest sister to wash the plates and dishes, while Rosamond cleaned up the hearth and swept the floor.

'I'm afraid I would more likely be a Mrs Nobbs than a Mrs Chaney,' Rica said, distastefully turning the earthenware about with shrinking fingers in the hot, greasy water. 'This fag of cleaning up after every meal is really sickening.'

'A useful poor man's wife you'd make!' Rosamond said. She stood at the door to shake the tablecloth into the garden, and the men, smoking at the gate, heard the speech.

'You forget,' said Eustace, turning round upon her, 'that Rica has never been as strong as a horse as you are, nor,' his eye moving over the girl's fine figure with an air of depreciation, 'does she look it.'

'Also her face is not heated to a lively crimson, and she has not judged it necessary to enhance her charms with a black smudge extending from the bridge of her nose to her right ear,' Tony added.

'That's so like a man!' cried Rosamond, with fierce derision. 'You work your fingers to the bone for him, and he talks to you about the softness of the hands of Mrs So-and-So, who always sits with them folded before her.'

CHAPTER SIX

'No Better than a Set of Gipsies'

'WHERE are you going?' Tony asked, when, an hour later, her hair free again about her face, her sailor hat on her head and *the* basket in her hand, she and the children passed him, aimlessly sauntering, near the cottage gate.

'We are going,' explained Bel, with eager satisfaction, 'to steal apples out of daddy's orchard.'

'Won't he be in a flightfully fuyous temper when he knows?' Bay demanded with glee.

'I'm going to steal them for to-morrow's pudding,' Rosamond explained.

'A method of spending the Sabbath afternoon that will scarcely commend itself to the sense of rectitude of our Eustace,' Tony reminded her.

'It is quite in the programme. What should the labourers' children do on Sunday afternoons but steal apples? – there being apples anywhere at hand to steal.'

'I'm not the village constable,' Tony said, and with drooped head and idly-rounded shoulders lounged on.

'Ah, melancholy moon calf!' the girl apostrophised him, looking after his long, limber figure with disapproving, wistful eyes. Then, with the little ones, filled with a delightful sense of wrong-doing, galloping beside her, she ran off across the meadow, and through the farmyard, and past the back of the farmhouse now occupied by Mr Dexter, the steward, and so made her way to the orchard.

All the trees there, save one, proved to be of the late-bearing kind, and in the month of August the fruit of this tree, even, was found to be of a woody, uninviting species; but the children robbed the lower branches, and threw stones and sticks, even the sacred basket itself, at the apples on the topmost ones, with an ecstasy of quaking delight.

On an ordinary Sunday afternoon, to go down with nurse to pick up the windfalls in the orchard at Bunwick was an agreeable diversion, perhaps, although quite permissible; being little cottage girls, and the occupation unlawful, it held strange attraction.

'If a policeman was to come!' Bel cried with a delicious shudder.

'And to bling us up before daddy!' Bay ejaculated, with ecstatic jumps. 'Would he order off our heads?' she inquired of her sister.

She thought her father, as J.P., had unlimited power in the matter of hangings and head-choppings; but she stood in none the more awe of him. She was afraid of no one and nothing in her safe little life. Everyone loved her. She firmly believed that the birds sang so loudly in the early morning to call her awake. Sometimes, intently listening, she could hear them say her name – 'Bay – Bay Boyan! Bay Boyan!' The moon looked in at her window at night because it was a friendly moon with a special liking for Bay. The daisy, her favourite as well as Nature's, grew in such abundance because she liked it best.

'It is nice to be one, but it is ext'ally delicious to be two,' she said, when, their labour over, they sat in the orchard grass, their basket of apples at their feet.

'One of you at a time is an ample sufficiency,' said the eldest girl. 'What do you mean by being two?'

'To be the little girl at the Hall and the little girl at Chelly-t'ee Cottages.'

'But you aren't,' said Rosamond, who loved to tease. 'You're little Bay Brunton, and nothing more. Bay Boyan isn't here any longer. She's vanished. I don't know in the least where Bay Boyan is.'

'But I want Bay Boyan's dolly, Maude,' the child said, the colour rushing to her chubby face.

'As if a little cottage girl could have a great beautiful doll and doll's house and a pram! You shall have the half of a pair of scissors if I can find it for you, and a broken bottle and a rusty door-key. You've got your hands to dig with in the dirt, and if you look about in the sand-pit you'll find some funny stones and shells to make gardens with.'

Whereupon a darkness and a blankness fell upon the child's small soul – her lip quivered, she got up, and, her hair tossing about her face, ran wildly round and round in order to conceal from Rosamond the fact that she wished to cry.

They spread the cloth for tea upon the meadow grass, beneath the big ash tree which stood at the corner of Mrs Nobbs's neglected garden. That good woman, coming out to empty a basin of warm, dirty water over the flower-bed, saw the preparations in progress, and the smoke ascending from the fire of sticks on which the kettle stood to boil. Mrs Nobbs had never beheld such goings-on on a Sunday afternoon. 'No better than a set of gipsies,' she declared. She was Conservative to the backbone, and did not approve of innovation. If you wanted a little outing on a Sunday, Mrs Nobbs was of the opinion there was no more agreeable and estimable mode of enjoying it than to go and sit for an hour or so with your man in the public-house, baby in his perambulator continuing to take the air at the door.

In the pleasurable excitement of feeding the fire with sticks, the children forgot to regret that particularly fascinating cake, with cherries in it and white sugar on the top, which was habitually their portion for Sunday tea. But how good the bread and butter was, even though stuck pretty closely with a tiny black-winged insect, with which the air beneath the ash tree swarmed that hot afternoon; and the tea, with its smoky flavouring, was delicious.

'The pound of butter which was to have lasted the week is finished,' Rosamond announced to Tony, when, Eustace and Rica having wandered away by themselves, she began to busy herself about clearing away the tea-things. 'Every penny of the three-and-sixpence in my purse will have to go for bread –'

'There is the pork dripping,' he reminded her.

'Flavoured by your tobacco ash. Enough to take us over to-morrow, perhaps.'

'Sufficient for the day,' suggested Tony.

'And there is always credit,' Rosamond reminded herself; 'but for that blessed provision I should throw up the game and run home, rather than watch the slow dissolution of my relatives by starvation.'

'Well, let's enjoy this perfect evening if we die to-morrow,' Tony said. He leant his back against the ash tree and slowly filled his pipe; the little girls, hugging their knees after their favourite fashion, leant against him, one on either side. 'Don't clatter the teacups, Rosamond. Be still and listen to the stillness,' he said.

'It's because it's Sunday,' Bel said, who was very susceptible of outward influence. She recognised with an awe past speech that sobering Sabbath stillness which lay upon Nature herself. The very sparrows chirped here and there with a different and subdued tone. The buzz of the insects floating on the drowsy air held something of decorum. The serenity of the cloudless sky spoke of a peace so limitless as to be heart-breaking; while the church bell, clanging loudly, and answered, sadly as an echo, by the neighbouring village steeples, called to the little girls with a reproachful inquiry why they sat on the grass at Tony Patten's feet instead of going to church to say their prayers as Eustace and his wife were going.

Bel, sitting in silence, with her mother far away, felt her heart sink and her conscience uncomfortably stir. She began to repent of having stolen her daddy's apples, and she wondered if it would be honourable in her, and something to appease the anger of that dread Power beyond the illimitable blue, if she refused apple dumpling for dinner to-morrow.

By the stillness and the solemn sweetness some sense of someone's responsibility was awakened in Tony, perhaps, for, looking up after a prolonged and thoughtful silence, –

'I should think it would be only decent if Rosamond went to church,' he said.

Rosamond was on her knees tying the plates and cups and saucers (they were of blue and white earth, and practically unbreakable) into a bundle in the tablecloth.

'Then carry in this bundle,' said Rosamond, 'wash up the tea-things, hear the children say their prayers, and put them to bed –'

('Oh, Tony, do!' the two little ones cried together, clutching him in ecstasy.)

'– gather the sticks for to-morrow's fire, fill the kettle ready for breakfast, make your own bed, which, I suppose, you didn't make this morning, and which I have forgotten till this minute. Will you do these things?'

'No, I won't,' said Tony, flatly. 'I am a lodger and an agricultural labourer, not a household slave.'

'Very well,' said Rosamond, energetically tying the corners of her bundle across and across, 'then don't preach.'

She slung the bundle upon her arm, and walked away with it, disdaining further speech. Her dark brown hair, which hung a heavy mass over her shoulders and down her back, had touches of red in it in that light; her dress was short enough to escape the heads of the buttercups and the daisies and the little dry plantain heads through which her feet passed with such a pleasant, rustling sound. She was tall, and had the grace which comes of physical freedom and perfect health and the beauty of harmonious proportion. As she walked over the meadow homeward, her bundle on her arm, her thoughts, 'pleasant as roses in the thicket blown,' were not occupied at all with her appearance on that Sabbath evening, but she made an agreeable picture for all that. Tony turned his head and watched her till she disappeared within the house, then he looked down upon the children on either side of him. 'Rosamond's got a temper of her own, hasn't she?' he remarked.

'She's my favourite of all,' said Bel, who was nothing if she was not loyal. 'Mary's my favourite always, and Rica's my favourite most often. Who's your favourite, Tony? Mary?'

'Mary – sometimes,' the young man confessed with a flicker of the lip. He knocked out the ashes of his pipe upon the roots of the tree by which he was sitting, and refilled it in silence, and silently began to smoke.

'You're my favourite of favourites,' Bay informed him, squeezing closer.

'Oh, come! What do you want?' he asked.

She wanted a story – a story about a dolly, please, the flatterer said, and dragged herself upon his outstretched legs to sit there, and laid her head back against his waistcoat.

What did they suppose there was in his career which should prompt him to burden his mind with histories of dollies, he inquired; and was told that on Sunday evenings Bay always stayed at home from church

38

because once in a day was enough for such a little girl; and mother stayed at home too, in order to tell her youngest daughter tales of dollies.

And, strange to say, Tony remembered that Bay's mother had told him a tale of a dolly too; which tale he could repeat to them if he liked; it was all he knew.

Was it a true tale?

Yes, as true as life and death, which were very true things, as even little girls knew.

A sad tale?

That depended on how you looked at things. Some people might laugh at it.

Bay liked the laughing ones best.

This was very laughing, then.

Supposing he, Tony Patten, were to play with a doll – would not Bay, and Bel too, laugh then? Supposing he kissed it, and talked to it, dressed and undressed it, and would not be parted from it, what would they do?

Bay giggled hysterically into his waistcoat at the idea. 'I should *loar* with laughing,' she said.

Tony did not wonder. And suppose an old, old woman, bent double, with white, white hair, and wrinkled hands that shook upon everything they touched – supposing she played with a doll like a little girl?

'We should die with laughing,' Bel declared.

'I thought you'd think it funny,' Tony said. Well, no farther off than the workhouse in the next parish this sight was to be seen, their mother had assured him. She had told him that when at Christmas she took the other old women presents of cake, of tea, of snuff, for this amusing old soul each year, at her own request, she carried a doll.

'Didn't mother loar with laughing?' Bay wanted to know.

Tony did not remember that she had laughed much. Yet to see all the other old women sitting, grumpy and complaining, over the fire, this with a back that ached, and that with feet that never were warm, and all with tales to tell of long lives, full of anxiety and hard work to end in the workhouse at last; and then to see this oldest of all among them, happy, with the doll in her lap, chatting to it, rocking it to sleep, putting it to bed on her pillow, where her eyes would fall on it as she woke in the morning – this certainly seemed very funny!

Had she loved her doll like that ever since she was a little girl? Bel asked.

Tony thought not so. He thought there had probably been an interlude in which her heart and her arms had been filled with other things.

Bay had suddenly become very still and grave. 'I shall love Dolly Maude all my life, too,' she said.

Bel turned her head and critically considered the narrative. 'I don't find it such a very funny story after all,' she said at length. 'Mother makes up much more *laughing* tales to tell us on Sunday evenings.'

'But this one is true,' asserted Tony. 'That is where the joke comes in.'

CHAPTER SEVEN

A Thin White Line

IT seemed to Rosamond, tired with her day's labours, that she had not been in bed half an hour when she was awakened by Rica standing in her nightdress at the bedside (they had not cumbered themselves with dressing-gowns at the cottage) and calling upon her to get up. She heard with bewildered unreadiness. She had never felt so in love with bed in her life as on that morning.

'It is five o'clock. Eustace is dressing; he has called Tony, who is now at the pump. In a few minutes they must be off. They want their breakfast, Rosamond.'

'Oh,' said Rosamond, unwillingly comprehending. Her pillow seemed magnetic, it was hard to drag her head from it. Slowly she sat up and pushed her loose hair from her eyes, and found that the sun was shining gaily through her open, uncurtained window, and the birds loudly singing in noisy greeting of the day.

She yawned and stretched her arms above her head, turned round and thumped her pillow, proving once more the soft delight of the refuge she was leaving, then put her feet upon the floor.

'You go back to bed,' she said to Rica, who shivered in the fresh morning air, 'I will give them their breakfasts.'

Rica threw a reproachful glance. 'As if I should lie comfortably in bed when my darling old Eustace has to go forth to work!' she said. 'If he has to rough it, so will I.'

'You aren't made of the right stuff for roughing it,' Rosamond said.

Indeed Rica, with her fair, fluffy hair about her little face, her large blue eyes still faint with sleep, looked as young as Rosamond, almost a child, and far more helpless.

'What are you going to give them for breakfast?' she asked, and was told that bread would be their portion – bread spread with the delicious dripping from yesterday's pork.

'But, Rosamond,' the wife complained, her eyes opening imploringly upon her sister, 'how is Eustace to work from half-past five in the morning until noon on bread and dripping?'

Why Eustace less than the rest? she was reminded. It was what they all had.

Then Rica, sitting on the side of the bed in which her little sisters were still sleeping, set forth, with hesitation and with blushes, the statement that her own appetite was extremely small, that her pet aversion in the way of eatables was pork. 'Couldn't I give up my slice at dinner, Rosamond, and let it go to Eustace?'

So between the slices of bread a piece of meat was put, and the sandwich, wrapped in a red handkerchief spotted white (they had carefully provided themselves with that pattern), stowed away in the Reverend Eustace's pocket.

'I wonder if I shall ever love a man well enough to give up my dinner for him?' Rosamond asked of herself, but asked aloud.

Eustace and his wife were saying a few last words beside the dew-drenched marigolds in the little garden. Tony's portion of bread and dripping was being placed in his handkerchief.

'I certainly expected you to relinquish your share of pork in favour of me,' he informed the girl.

'Which shows what mistakes an otherwise intelligent young man may make when he is carried away by the exuberance of his own vanity,' Rosamond told him.

The women walked with their menkind along the meadow roadway and through the nearly empty stackyard, and picked their way over a road deep-lined with ruts of cart wheels, broken down, and mended with old bricks, with rubbish of all kinds, where, even in a drought such as was prevailing now, mud was churned up on all sides. Here was the big barn, about whose doors the workmen assembled every morning of their lives to receive their orders from Mr Dexter, the steward, who, seated on the low plank which guarded the entrance to the open barn, his eyes upon the rough ground at his feet, in the slow tones of stolid indifference, allotted to each man his day's work.

The girls stopped where they would be unobserved by the little crowd, and watched the two men join the group. They waited until first one then another labourer, spitting on the earth he was to till as the only comment on his instructions, turned, listlessly slouching away; then, for fear of discovery in their lurking-place, they made off homeward.

'I so hope Dexter will give Eustace something that is not really hard work!' his wife said anxiously.

'You may depend upon it, whatever they give him will seem hard to Eustace,' Rosamond assured her. 'But you may be also quite certain it won't hurt him.'

—※◆※—

The children rebelled against their porridge for breakfast. For one thing, no milk was procurable (Mrs Dexter did not understand a dairy, and cows were not kept at the farm); for another, Rosamond, who had no proper saucepan to use, contrived to burn the oatmeal, and Rica declared they could not afford to throw it away. To each a portion was sternly doled out, therefore; but when Bay was seen to be silently weeping into her plate, Rosamond relented, and toasted a stack of bread slices which, spread with dripping, the children ate ravenously.

'It seems such a shame for us to gobble it alone! It is the sort of thing Eustace would so much enjoy,' Rosamond bemoaned.

So Mrs Chaney's seven chickens, which ran in and out of a coop beneath the garden fence, and endlessly picked and scraped the meadow grass, came in for the burnt oatmeal. Indeed, during the week of the Patten Experiment, Mrs Chaney's chickens fared better than they were ever likely to do again until that, by them, not-altogether-to-be-desired period arrived when they should be fatted for table.

The children went off in a body to school, the Boyans being accompanied by the four clean little boys and girls from the cottage on the right and the six dirty ones from the cottage on the left.

Rica, looking upon the latter as they issued from their gate, called to her own little sisters, spick and span in their scarlet overalls, their brown hair, so bright and tenderly cared for, flowing beneath their sun-hats.

'Don't go near them, don't touch them,' Rica commanded in a horrified whisper. 'You may be kind to them, but keep as far away as you can.'

'I can't think how mother can have consented to the little ones going to school,' she said, watching the departure with apprehensive eyes. 'Among that crew they look like creatures of another world.'

'Mother thinks good may come of it,' Rosamond explained. 'It isn't because it is your Eustace's last fad that she is consenting to this, but because she thinks good may come.'

'Very horrid things may come too, in my opinion,' Rica dolefully said.

'In which case we have only Eustace to thank,' Rosamond reminded her.

In the course of the morning Rosamond carried out a pail to the rain water tub, which stood beside her own cottage door and was the common property of Cherry-tree Row. She mounted the block of wood on which the tub was fixed, and, leaning over its side, looked upon the dark, malodorous water within. Instantly the door upon her left hand was flung noisily open, and Mrs Nobbs, her rough, grey hair flying about her yellow, not unyouthful, face, her rusty black gown bursting away from its fastenings across the bust and its moorings to the skirt, accosted the girl in tones at once sullen and shrill.

'That there water's for the washin' o' clo'es,' she cried. 'I take it you ha'n't got no clo'es to wash as you ha'n't been here long enough to dirty 'em.'

The water looked as black as ink, and there were not more than a dozen pints, but Rosamond conceived that it behoved her to stand up for her rights.

'I don't intend to explain to you for what purpose I draw the water,' therefore she remarked. 'You'll find we use a good deal, because, as it happens, we're people who like to be clean.'

'Then you'll please to fetch it from the pump,' her antagonist screamed at her; 'and you'd best make spare o' that, for there ain't a summer it don't go dry, and there ain't a winter it ain't froze up. This here's my washin' day,' she volunteered, and flinging into the house, she flung forth again with a dirty pail, into which, by means of a bowl, scooping the dark fluid from the bottom of the tub, she emptied the precious water.

Having elbowed Rosamond from her position and gained her point she became grudgingly amicable. 'Such as for scrubbin' o' bricks, and biling o' vegetables, there's the pump,' she condescended to explain.

'And suppose that I wish to wash linen to-day in ink-black, offensively smelling water?' queried Rosamond the indignant.

'That ain't none o' my business,' Mrs Nobbs replied, and was retiring into her cottage, sullenly triumphant, with her spoils, when the lattice window of the Chaneys' second floor opened, and Mrs Chaney, half her body thrown forward in mid-air, in the decent, restrained tones, which Mrs Nobbs had confessed to her husband had a more irritating effect on her nerves than the roaring of forty bulls, inquired if she weren't ashamed of herself demeaning herself before the young lady so?

Whereupon Mrs Nobbs, casting a scowling, disdainful glance upon her neighbour, called upon her if she'd got anything to say to come down and say it like a woman, and not to skulk up in her chamber like a bleating, black-faced yow, maunderin' on no one knew what.

Upon which Mrs Chaney, mildly remarking that her neighbour was a low-mouthed, disgraceful critter, closed her window and disappeared.

Later, this good woman came into the Boyans' cottage for the luxury of abusing the common enemy.

''Tis her graspin', greedy sperrit, miss; 'taint no wash as she's a-goin' to do,' she explained. 'Why, the last time as the tub were full, Mrs Brunton she'd set her mind to a wash, and was a-holdin' forth on the beautiful soft water she'd have in plenty – what do this here critter do but to pull the tap out over night, so when the po'r woman come to heat her water for the wash there weren't a drop!'

'I shall speak to the steward about her,' Rosamond said.

'My dear! – excusin' me with makin' so free – that ain't a mite o' good. Nobbs he've got his discharge and go to his work three mile distant. That's what make her so uppish.'

'Not even water enough!' Rica cried when she heard of the probability of the pump going dry.

But across the meadow, in that little fenced-off portion of land where the old cottages had stood, and where Mr Boyan had arranged allotments for his men (which allotments since the first year had never been let), was a well, the sisters were told. However dry was the cottage pump, however long the drought, the water came up there, sparklin' like diamonds, Mrs Chaney assured them, and that ice-cold it stopped your breath.

So Rica decided that that would be the most grateful drink for the men coming home hot and thirsty to dinner. They had not greatly enjoyed water as a dinner beverage yesterday, but that might have been because it came from a nearly dry pump. While Rosamond made her preparations for dinner, therefore, Rica started, the bright zinc pail over her arm, to fetch water from the well in the allotments.

The field beyond the gently-sloping meadow and the narrow tree-bordered road was planted with turnips that year. It was a space of about twenty-four acres, and rose gradually to the horizon line. As Rica emerged from the front gate of the cottage she saw, conspicuous in their white shirt-sleeves in the blazing sunshine, a half-dozen men – a thin white line in the shadowless expanse – busy, hoe in hand, singling the young plants.

Rica stood still for a moment, motionless with dismay, then rushed back to the house.

'Rosamond! oh, Rosamond!' she cried; and her cries were those of anguish, so that Rosamond, starting violently over the slicing of the potatoes, sliced her thumb as well. 'Here is Eustace, Rosamond! Oh, come and see.'

The girl swaddled her bleeding thumb in her handkerchief and flew to the door. 'Unless you've found his mutilated corpse somewhere you aren't justified in making such a to-do,' she cried.

But Rica was pointing across the meadow, where the grass was baking in the intemperate noon, to the field where the men in their shirt-sleeves were working under the pitiless sun. The brothers were distinguishable by the white flannel trousers they wore.

'It will kill him,' Rica said with a dreadful calm. 'The least sun on the back of his neck gives him the headache. How mean and spiteful of Dexter to give him such a task!'

'Why is he better than the others?' Rosamond demanded with contempt. She unwound her bleeding finger and showed it to her sister. 'That's what you've done with your screams for "Rosamond"!' she said.

Rica cast indifferent eyes upon the wound and looked back to her martyr in the turnip field.

'When you have a husband of your own you won't ask why he is better,' she said with resigned superiority. 'You'll know there's no one in the whole world who signifies in comparison.'

Then, moved by the pathos of her words, she began to cry openly. 'You are unfeeling because you don't know what it is to love anyone as I love Eustace,' she said, and with a sob she clutched her pail again and walked away.

'If I'm to be such a fool when I marry, may Heaven keep me to the end an old maid,' Rosamond piously ejaculated as she looked after her.

CHAPTER EIGHT

The Wrong End of the Stick

IT was not till the noon hour that Rica returned, and then she came accompanied by her husband, who was supporting her with his arm about her waist, and Tony, who carried the pail of water.

'You have been gone two mortal hours to fetch a pail of water,' Rosamond told her sister.

'She should never have been sent for it,' her husband announced in tones of displeasure, and he cast a very haughty glance at Rosamond through his glasses. His own face, the back of his neck, his ears were crimson from the sun; as he threw off his cap it was seen that his hair was matted upon his forehead, from which, now and again, a drop trickled and dropped on to the floor.

'You who have been sitting comfortably at home don't know how confoundedly hot it is,' Tony said, and he also adopted the voice of censure.

'If I had been "comfortably sitting," where do you imagine your apple-dumpling would have been?' the girl demanded with natural indignation.

'As a matter of fact, where is it?' the young man inquired. 'Eustace and I feel uncommonly peckish, I can tell you, Rosamond.'

He tossed his cap on to the peg behind the door, and calling to the children to work the handle for him, went and placed his head beneath the pump.

'It is only that I have the headache,' said Rica. 'It was the glare of the sun in my eyes. I think if I go upstairs and lie down for half an hour I shall be all right, dear.'

So Eustace, with his hands on the back of her waist, gently helping her ascent, accompanied his wife to their room, and having laid her on the bed, and pinned a towel across the unprotected window to keep out the cruel sun, sat beside her holding her hand, nursing dark thoughts in his mind the while against that iniquitous person who had set his darling such a task to perform.

Rica faintly excused her sister.

'It is sweet of you, darling, but the fact remains. Rosamond acted selfishly. It was selfish in her to sit at home comfortably peeling apples, and to send you, who have not a quarter of her strength, on such an errand.'

46

'But you mustn't be angry, Eustace. You must remember that no one cares for me as you do.'

In these first days of rapturous enjoyment of the mere fact of belonging to each other, they had almost persuaded themselves, so transcendent was their affection each for each, that no one belonging to them had any affection at all; and each fought the other's battles as if the family circle were a society of cruel enemies from whom the beloved object had to be jealously protected.

Except a crust of bread and a drink of the spring water which Tony had carried home, nothing had Rica for her dinner. Her husband fetched her those delicacies, maintaining as he did so an air of injured reserve and haughty disapproval. When, finally, he took his place at the board, he regarded the steaming pudding and the heaped plates of the rest with a condemnatory and gloomy stare. With Rica suffering, how could they eat of the delicacies of the season!

Truth to say, if they had not been so hungry, the dinner would not have been found appetising. As it was, however, they ate their food almost entirely without comment. Indeed, so touchy was Rosamond on the subject of her cooking, which, truth to say, left something to desire, that they found it wiser to refrain from criticism.

Tony, indeed, in the small voice of timidity, ventured to mention that, in his opinion, the pudding would have been more successful if the apples had been *cooked*. After which he fell back, apparently lifeless, in his chair.

'It was fortunately only a glance she threw at me,' he explained to Bel, who flew to him, wondering. 'If it had been knives they could not have been discharged with more direful vengeance.'

'It seems to me Tony had better change his lodgings,' Rosamond said, also addressing Bel, her dignity not allowing her to stoop to a conversation with the young man himself. 'He would be welcomed, I have no doubt, by neighbours on either hand. I know what both of them are having for their dinner to-day. I had the curiosity to go in to see. I borrowed half a pound of sugar of Mrs Chaney, and I carried a dozen apples as a present to Mrs Nobbs. Mrs Chaney had on her table dumplings like those we had yesterday – they were eating them with a little pepper and salt, and butter added to the water they were boiled in.'

'Don't!' said Tony, putting up his hand. 'Hold! I feel ill.'

'And the Nobbses have a great basin of watery potatoes and bread, and nothing else –'

'While Tony, who with his enormous appetite has to be fed and boarded on the paltry sum of less than a shilling a day which he pays us, thanks to my father's apple trees and to my industry, has delicious pudding first and potatoes to follow.'

'And aren't we, who have earned everyone's living by the sweat of our brows, to taste meat to-day, then?' Tony inquired.

And Eustace, looking severely upon the trifler, said sharply, 'No!' He stuck out his jaw at Tony in silence for a minute or two. 'Who are we that we should fare better than the rest?' he demanded.

'By care and extremely good management great things can be done,' said Rosamond, and she looked at Tony while her eyelashes fluttered rapidly for a second on her cheek.

('You do that because you daren't wink,' said Tony, quickly, watching the pretty trick; at which she showed him that she dared.)

'I find my neighbours make it a rule that the breadwinners have meat once a day, but as we are all workers – even the children who go backwards and forwards to school, even I, who sit at my elegant ease and peel potatoes, even Rica, who – I really don't know how Rica works –'

'In future I forbid you to send Rica upon any such errand as that of this morning,' Eustace said, with biting distinctness, glowering upon his sister-in-law. 'She was staggering, positively staggering, beneath the weight of the water, the sun beating on her. A little of that sort of thing would kill Rica,' he added with a challenging look around. He was immensely proud of his wife's feebleness.

'She shall be wrapped in cotton-wool, but she shall have her slice of meat a day all the same,' Rosamond promised.

—❊❖❊—

Josher Nobbs was such a darling little boy, might she bring him in to tea? Bay was heard anxiously enquiring.

Her request was promptly refused. Josher was far too dirty. She might introduce a little Chaney, who, at any rate, had a surface cleanliness. But this suggestion was without charm for Bay. The youngest Chaney was in knickerbockers; it was the petticoat of Joshua which appealed to Bay.

Bel explained that Josher was not a boy, in her opinion, to compare with Ivan Cattle, who sat next her in school. Ivan was much bigger than Bel; but, although so desirable a lad in other respects, his deficiency in book learning held him still among the little ones in the third standard. He had pinched his new neighbour's arm till it was black and blue, Bel proudly explained, and pulled up her loose sleeve in proof that she told no lie. He had pulled her hair, too, in such a clever way that although she, taken unawares, screeched out once or twice, Governess had never suspected the malpractices of solemn-faced Ivan. Indeed, Isabel was quite eloquent on the subject of Master Cattle, and was anxious to get back to school that she might sit next the dear, ingenious youth again.

Poor Josher, being too small to toddle backwards and forwards, had stayed at school to dinner, Bay informed them. Not much was in his dinner bag, only the outside dried crust of a loaf of bread upon which a little lard had been spread.

'And very nice, too!' Rosamond declared staunchly. She had a new sympathy with harassed mothers of hungry households. 'With eleven shillings a week and six children to keep, will you please say how you are going to allow Joshua more?'

'But–' said the Reverend Eustace, slowly. He paused there, gazing at the subject through his glasses. 'The question is, is a crust of bread and a smearing of grease a sufficient meal for Joshua?' he concluded.

'It's a question which does not seem to trouble Joshua's mother,' Rosamond told him.

The clergyman thoughtfully stuck out his jaw. 'It's a question Joshua's country will have to trouble about one day, I think,' he said.

Then he went upstairs again to his wife and sat beside her in her darkened room for the remainder of the mid-day rest.

The children went off gaily to school, Bay made happy by the possession of a hard green apple which she destined for an offering to Josher. Bel declined the opportunity of making a like gift to her hero. Ivan was a boy who would scorn to have an apple presented to him while he could rob an orchard, she knew.

'Aren't you going to help me clean up?' Rosamond demanded in an injured voice of Tony, disappearing, by way of the front room, through the open door.

'Aren't you going to help me hoe my turnips?' Tony retorted, pausing a minute to feel in the pocket of his discarded jacket for his pipe and tobacco.

The girl looked after him wistfully as he walked down the little garden path between the tall red and white phloxes and past the delphiniums. He stopped by the enormous sun-flower at the gate, its head a foot above his own tall one. His spare, supple figure showed to the best advantage in his loose white flannel shirt and trousers, girt about the waist with a handkerchief gay with his college colours.

'What splendid form he is in!' Rosamond said to herself, admiringly. She took the deepest pride in his prowess as an athlete. Her father had not ceased to laugh at her yet because she had shed tears last year when the young man had been beaten at the hurdle race where he had always come in first before.

She watched him while he lit his pipe beneath the sun-flower, bending his head to the flame protected in his curved hands, then, lounging through the little gate, sat down with a sigh of content beneath the palings and contemplated the meadow spread before him, defenceless in the broiling sunshine.

In the kitchen, where was Rosamond's sphere, was distasteful work to be done, dirt, discomfort. There were the dinner things to be cleared, those and the saucepan to be washed, the stove, when the fire was dying down, to be cleaned. In the freshness of her morning feeling Rosamond had announced that she meant to scrub the bricks and to clean the doorstep that afternoon. But these contemplated tasks had grown loathsome – and the sun shone dazzlingly on the garden flowers, and Tony sat and smoked his pipe alone.

She suddenly remembered that Mrs Chaney's seven poor little chickens must not be neglected, and, having scooped the crumbs from the table into her apron, she carried them out to the little brood on the meadow, and sat down in the sunshine by Tony's side.

'And how is poor little Rica?' he inquired pityingly.

'Why is she "poor little Rica"? She is taller than I am. She has the best of everything. She is petted from morning till night. She has been from her cradle and will be to her grave. "Rica mustn't do this!" "Rica mustn't do that!" Here am I, slaving for you all –'

'You don't forget to mention the fact, my dear.'

'There is the work of six women waiting to be done this afternoon –'

'I wouldn't waste time about beginning.'

'Does anyone say "poor little Rosamond"?'

'It's because Rica's so pretty,' he suggested, with a sidelong glance at her.

'And I'm so ugly, I suppose?'

He smoked on in silence.

'Thank you,' she said, with a very red face, her chin up.

She had always been comfortably assured that she was not ugly, but Tony's taste was peculiar in many instances. It was quite possible she seemed so to him. Her thoughts flew away, as they had a trick of doing when her vanity was hurt, to Alan Mason, he who had made the collection of hairpins, and whose admiration of his friend Dolly's third sister had been quite unconcealed.

'You don't know Mr Alan Mason, I think?' she inquired with polite interest. 'Oh, you needn't shake your head in that hasty and contemptuous manner. He is quite as interesting as – other people, I assure you, and much better looking than most. He is not exactly clever, perhaps –'

'Dear me! I am surprised to hear it.'

'Not like Eustace, for instance, but, on the other hand, he does not pretend to be. By the way, have you ever heard Eustace say a clever thing in his life? I never have. He is always telling you how clever he is –'

'What a crammer!'

'Oh, not in so many words, perhaps; what are words when you can convey an impression? Why doesn't he favour us once in a moonshine with an example? But Alan Mason said one very true thing.'

'It is better to be truthful than clever.'

'He said, "Cambridge men pride themselves on nothing so much as their bad manners."'

'You must be awfully pleased your brother Dolly was sent to Oxford,' Tony said, and Rosamond digested that remark in silence; for Dolly ('the dearest, the most darling boy in the world'), still in his first year at Oxford, was certainly lacking a little in polish just at present.

She scattered a crumb or two to the clustering, fluffy chickens at her feet.

'You can't understand,' she said thoughtfully, 'how delightful it is for a girl – even such a young girl as I am – to associate with a man who is not ashamed to be polite.'

'Naturally it is a matter beyond my comprehension.'

'That was why Mr Alan Mason and I got on so beautifully together. He's got Dolly over at his place now, you know, but I suppose he will be with us again before the end of the holidays.'

'It would be an education to know him. I hope he'll come before I leave,' Tony said. He had selected a stiff plantain stalk and was trying to insert it into the stem of his pipe, which did not draw to his satisfaction. 'Poor little Rica, you know!' he said, placidly reverting to his original theme. 'She actually lugged that bucket of spring water all the way from the well across the turnips to us. Half of it was spilt. Her clothes on one side were drenched. She was half dead with heat and fatigue.'

'What an idiot!' said Rosamond.

'The men, when they caught sight of her, thought some beer was coming. They said a few things when they found it was only water (they had not been brought up at Oxford, you know). Not one of them would touch it. Of course she did not care, poor little girl. She had brought it for Eustace. He drank a lot, boiling hot as he was, to please her, and got a bad pain in his chest in consequence. He went and sat down under the hedge with Rica, and groaned till it was time to come home.'

'How could Rica have been such a silly?' Rosamond said, contemptuously laughing.

'Oh, well,' said Tony, poking away at the pipe stem, 'I think it was very pretty of her. I'd just give half the years of my life to have a woman care for me like that! Only you'd better have an eye to her, Rosamond. You mustn't let her run after him into the fields where the other men are. It gives rise to a show of wit on their part a little trying to her connections by marriage.'

'I will do what I can,' said Rosamond, suddenly very docile and soft of voice. She turned her head, leaning back a little, as she sat beside him, and secretly contemplated his clean, sun-baked cheek and strong, bare throat. The close-cut dark hair, which grew straight and black upon his head, clung, closely curling, to nape and brow on this hot afternoon. Of course someone would be found who loved him as he wished, the girl said to herself, with a wistful, motherly sadness. Was it likely Tony would wish and wish in vain when Eustace had had what he wanted for the asking? Eustace, the lank and lean, the sallow-faced, lantern-jawed! Rosamond sighed to think how easily he could have his will; yet she wanted things to go pleasantly with Tony.

He had pushed the grass to the bowl of his pipe, and was busy fishing for the end with his penknife, intent on no other thought than effecting the free passage he desired. Rosamond, edging a little closer to him, looked over his shoulder.

'Tony,' she whispered in a small voice, 'you remember what I told you about Mary yesterday?'

'Mary? Well?'

'Of course I can't be certain how Mary feels about that little man. She never actually told me. I only guessed. I may be quite wrong, Tony.'

He might have been very much relieved, he might have been perfectly indifferent, she could not tell. In either case he spoke no word.

'You haven't got a pair of tweezers about you, have you?' presently he asked. 'I can't catch hold of this confounded thing.'

He suddenly tired of the attempt, flung the plantain stalk upon the grass, and sprang to his feet.

'It isn't time for you to go yet, Tony? When Chaney goes –'

'Chaney is a married man and I'm a free one,' he reminded her. Then he plunged his hands into the pockets of his white trousers and rattled the loose coin there. 'Family affections and family joys perhaps make up to Chaney for a habitual insufficiency of nourishment. I have not those agreeable substitutes for a full and sufficient meal. And, truth to tell, I am conscious of an unpleasant vacuum –'

He untied the red and black silk handkerchief about his waist, and pulled it tight, drawing in his breath. It seemed to Rosamond, alarmedly watching, that he was going to cut himself in two with it before her eyes.

'A pipe doesn't fill the void,' he explained, smiting that part of his person where the void was situated with his open hand; 'the charms of your society and the contemplation of the pure pleasures of rural life don't fill it, Rosamond. I am going to try what beer will do. I am going to visit the village pub.'

Rosamond looked after the young man as, with his red and black striped cap on the back of his head, his hands in his pockets, he sauntered away. Then she turned back, past the phloxes and the gay garden flowers, flagging a little in the pitiless sun, through the smart front room with the smell of its highly-varnished deal chairs very heavy in the air that hot afternoon, to her tasks in the dirty, muddled-up kitchen beyond. She turned up the sleeves of her dark blue print, twisted the freely hanging hair into a tail, tied the tail in a knot, and switched it into place again.

'Daddy always says that women have got hold of the wrong end of the stick,' she soliloquised. 'I begin to think that, for once in his life, daddy is right.'

CHAPTER NINE

Mrs Dodman to Call

UPSTAIRS in the front bedroom, whose tiny window overlooked the meadow, and beyond the meadow that field of aching green which lay glistering in the afternoon sun, a tragic farewell was taking place.

Rica's head was no better, but the relentless call of duty must drag her husband from her side to resume his heavy toil.

'I hate to leave you like this, darling. But, however ill they are, your father's labourers have to leave their suffering wives or to sacrifice the day's wage. We can't afford to lose any of our eleven shillings, Rica.'

'I don't want to be selfish to keep you with me,' Rica said, clinging to the adored clergyman, 'but I hate to think of you *killing* yourself in the broiling sun, and after such a dinner, too! So horrid of Rosamond, who knows your weak digestion, not to see if the apples would cook before she put them in a pudding. Do you feel that pain still, dear?'

'It is pretty bad,' acknowledged the poor gentleman. 'But I don't think I feel so hungry as I should if I had not got the pain.'

'I think a mouthful of brandy neat would set me right,' he said to Rosamond on his way out. 'And a dash of brandy in some soda-water is just the thing Rica wants for her head.'

'And where do you suppose we are to get the dash of brandy?' Rosamond inquired derisively.

He had no reply to that question handy, and with a sigh he went on his way. He gave a lingering look at that shrouded window behind which his little Rica lay, and crossed the meadow and gained the field of his labours.

It was the best of weather for singling – no fear of the uprooted plants taking root again. Those that had been hoed up in the morning lay, shrunk and shrivelled, upon the baked grey soil; the leaves of the growing plants flagged beneath the glaring, cloudless sky. There was that curious flicker in the atmosphere which hurts the eyes to contemplate, and which we call heat visible. Nature herself seemed to be distressed and to pant in the hot air.

⁓⚜⁓

'There ain't no wash a-goin' on next door,' Mrs Chaney said, looking in upon Rosamond on her knees sweeping the grate. 'I told you she would ha' that water for the love o' gettin', miss. You'd best let on to her as you onderstand her ways.'

'Can't you do it for me, Mrs Chaney?' Rosamond asked. 'I've a good deal to do this afternoon, and my sister is ill upstairs.'

So Mrs Chaney, nothing loth, although her own afternoon work was yet to begin, threw her apron over her bare arms, walked across the open space at the back of the three cottages, and appeared at Mrs Nobbs's door.

'There's a butiful dry, but I don't see no linen a-hangin' out,' she said. She had to call the remark aloud, for Mrs Nobbs was not in the filthy kitchen. She was in the chamber above, it appeared, for presently the window over the door opened and the rough grey head and yellow face became visible.

'I was a-inquirin' how the wash was a-gettin' on this here butiful drying day, Mrs Nobbs,' the neighbour informed her in the suave and affable tones which had such a goading effect on the other woman.

'The wash is over and I'm a-throwin' out the dirty water,' said Mrs Nobbs. And with that – splash – she flung the contents of a basin she held at Mrs Chaney's head.

'I knowed the woman 'ud be up to them dirty tricks, and that's why I let on to her,' Mrs Chaney explained to Rosamond, coming in, leisurely rubbing her bare arms and the front of her dress with the coarse apron tied at her waist. 'I stepped back jest in time, or I'd ha' had to strip, maybe. 'Tis a pity she have sech a nasty, onneighbour'y ways.'

Then the good woman, without any invitation, made her way up to Rica. She stood at the foot of the sufferer's bed and talked for half an hour on the special suffering attached to different kinds of 'hids.'

She herself had a dizzy one, and could not stiddy herself to do her work, but went a-buzzin' round, wi' the cheers and tables a-skelterin' after her. Mrs Barrett at the shop was, for her part, afflicted wi' rheumaticky pains, her hid felt as big as a bushel skep, and you might hear her groan right acrost the road when she was at her worst. A sister of Mrs Chaney's own, at service, seed stars a-shootin' and a-dartin'; and there was yet another variety of hid, with which a cousin of Mrs Chaney's mother was afflicted, which caused her to look at everything through a mist.

It seemed to poor Rica, lying helpless upon her bed, and too courteous to show her visitor that the conversation added to her suffering, that she had not only her own headache to bear, but the headaches of all the variously-afflicted sufferers in the parish of Dulditch.

She fell asleep, worn out with suffering, when Mrs Chaney took her departure. But in less than half an hour the good soul was back again, having brewed, out of her own scanty store, a cup of tea for her poor young neighbour. She had cut a careful slice of bread and butter too, and Rica, awakening refreshed from her sleep, ate and drank and was better.

While Mrs Chaney thus delayed the commencement of her afternoon labours, and while Mrs Nobbs, on the other hand of her, sat in her filthy kitchen spelling out the lengthy report of a murder from the voluminous pages of the last week's *People's Chronicle*, Rosamond, struggling vigorously with those herculean labours which, in the best way she could, she must overcome, began to see the grateful end of her toil approaching. She had washed up saucepans and dinner things, had cleaned the stove, laid the fire ready to light, filled the kettle for tea. But she was not trained in such services, and it must be owned her methods were open to criticism. She had suffered in her person, too, considerably. She had spilt water upon her apron, rubbed soot upon her face and arms; in the ardent brown of her thick hair dust had settled, and on the crown of her head was a large flake of whitening, she having laid her head against the wall in her effort to clear out the oven.

She was proceeding with her last task, the sweeping of the kitchen floor, when Mrs Chaney, flurried and eager, appeared before the door again.

'Look out, miss,' she said, 'here be the new parson's wife a-comin' to the cottages.'

Now it happened, in this month of August, that the old Rector of Dulditch, whose health had been for some time breaking, had been ordered away for a change of air, his place being taken in pulpit and rectory by a clergyman from another county, with whom he had temporarily exchanged livings.

The new man and his wife, having only just arrived in the place, had begun in very energetic fashion, strongly in contrast with the loose methods of the old rector, to make a house-to-house visitation.

Mrs Dodman was unaccompanied by her husband on this occasion. She was a large, florid, untidy, not ill-looking woman; and of the three Cherry-tree Cottages she took that occupied by Mrs Nobbs first.

Mrs Nobbs, dirty, sullen, monosyllabic, was not an encouraging subject. She groped under the flat cushion of the fireside chair for the family pocket-handkerchief, always kept there, wiped with it the seat of the chair nearest the door, by the action inviting the visitor to sit there. The clergyman's wife, heated by her uphill tramp across the meadow, and short of breath, sat a minute in silence, gazing upon the unwashed plates, the dirty bricks, the untidy condition of the woman's iron-grey hair, with an expression of open disapprobation.

'This is a sad scene of poverty and neglect,' she said, having sufficiently taken in the details. 'What wages is your husband in receipt of, my good woman?'

'I don't know as that consarn only him and me,' the woman said. She added, in sulky apology for her reticence, that the walls was only lath and plaster, and neighbours always a-pokin' and a-pryin'. The woman next door, she said, nodding in the direction of the innocent Rosamond, had only to put her hid up th' chimley and she could hear ivery word that was spoke.

'Does not your neighbour know that to listen is dishonourable, and to show curiosity about other people's affairs is vulgar?' Mrs Dodman inquired.

And Mrs Nobbs replied discouragingly that she didn't know. It weren't nothin' to do with her.

Then the lady extracted from the leather bag hanging at her substantial waist a few leaflets, which she commended to the consideration of Mrs Nobbs, asking her when she should have read the pages to pass them about among her friends.

'Yer can lay them on the table,' said Mrs Nobbs, with a jerk of her head in the direction of that filthy piece of furniture.

'They are in favour of temperance,' the clergywoman said. 'I am a great advocate of it – of total abstinence, indeed – among the poor. If I could see it established everywhere, there would, indeed, be no poor – all of you would be happy, well-to-do – no untidy homes, no half-fed children, no slipshod, neglected wives.'

'No one to preach to,' said Mrs Nobbs. Since the lady's arrival she had set to work with obtrusive energy to tidy her room. She flung the broken chairs aside, as if they were so many enemies in her path, as she savagely swept the bricks.

'I beg your pardon, my good woman?' Mrs Dodman had lost the last remark in the clatter and confusion.

Mrs Nobbs paused on her knees, and lifted her sallow face to the intruder. 'How much drink do you think we get out of eleven shillings a week?' she demanded fiercely. 'Eight mouths to feed. Try it yourself and see what you've left to get drunk on.' She nodded to the papers on the table. 'Yer can take yer rubbage,' she said. 'Sech readin' ain't in my line. I ha'n't no time for it.'

The wife of the Reverend Christopher Dodman rose from her seat. 'Civility is not costly, my good woman,' she said. 'But I perceive there is much work still to do which should have been completed earlier in the day. I will not further interrupt you.'

'I ain't a-prayin' of you to stay alonger me,' the woman said. She picked up the rag of mat from the door, and, as the lady passed out, she shook it violently in her direction. So that, pursued by a cloud of dust, it was with the report of a loud, irrepressible sneeze that Mrs Dodman announced her arrival at Rosamond's door.

The door – it was against the back premises Mrs Dodman had directed her attack – stood open, and looking within, the lady saw a kitchen that, leaving something of orderliness to desire, was yet a model of cleanliness compared with that she had left. In the middle of it, pausing upon her interrupted work, stood a tall girl, leaning upon a long-handled broom.

Rosamond's eyes, as they encountered those of her visitor, held a doubtful expression. Had the stranger heard the tale of the Patten Experiment? In the vanity of her inexperienced youth, Rosamond was of opinion that, the story heard or no, it was not possible for any woman of breeding to mistake her, Rosamond Boyan, for one of the class by whom the Cherry-tree Cottages should be peopled.

Mrs Dodman's unspeculative eyes, a glassy blue in her expanse of florid face, gazed with some degree of approbation upon the young person before her. Here was a far more promising specimen, she thought. This creature was so young that she must be respectful, and also would probably be grateful for good advice.

'Good afternoon,' she said, and took the nearest chair, and cast questioning glances over the room. 'I am the wife of the clergyman in whose charge your good rector has temporarily left his parish. I think it my duty to make the acquaintance of all the parishioners. You are the eldest daughter of the good man of the house, I suppose?'

Rosamond regarded her with wary brown eyes across the top of the broom on which her hands were folded, and silently shook her head.

'Not the eldest? The eldest at home, then? Don't be afraid to speak out, my good girl. There is nothing to be afraid of. You are out of place for a time, perhaps?'

Again Rosamond shook her head.

'But you are far too big for your mother to keep at home doing nothing! How old are you?'

'I am seventeen,' said Rosamond, clearly, and watched the effect. Surely the woman would know by her voice and intonation that she was not one of the labourers' daughters.

But the woman was not of an observant species. In her scheme of society distinctions are drawn with a very hard line. You may find a George Eliot among the farming class, a Robbie Burns in his peasant dress may sing as he follows the plough, let such keep the places to which they were born. Mrs Dodman has probably never heard with conscious ears of one or the other. Of what has she heard beyond the borders of the parochial arena? She knows nothing of wit, of beauty, of genius, of the nobility of men's minds; nothing of the large claims of the human family, each member hanging upon each; nothing of the history of her own times; the advance of science is but a name to her, the region of letters is almost totally unexplored by her, the true meaning of life unguessed at. But with her own and her husband's narrow interpretation of the Christian doctrine she is acquainted, and performs the duties she

58

conceives to be hers rigorously in her limited sphere, being accounted among her 'set' a splendid clergyman's wife, and a good woman.

'And have you never been out to service?' she demanded of the fine-looking specimen of young humanity before her, who, leaning upon her broom, regarded her with challenging eyes. 'Dear me! That seems very remiss on the part of your mother. I daresay when I see her I shall hear the usual tale of poverty, complaints of the lowness of wages and the number of mouths to feed. Yet a great, hungry girl like you stays at home to eat the bread out of brothers' and sisters' mouths. Should you not wish to remove such a burden from your parents' shoulders, and to go forth and earn your own living as a respectable, well-conducted servant?'

Again Rosamond shook her head. 'I should not like it at all,' she said.

'I am sorry to hear you say so, for I have seen other girls like you dawdling at home with *the worst results.*'

'What results?' Rosamond inquired, bold in her innocence.

'Ah! That we need not go into. Being idle themselves they have contracted friendships with idle young men; they adopt a style of dress quite unbecoming their station in life; it is all very painful. You will forgive my saying I consider the fashion in which your hair is hanging down your back most improper. A neat twist at the back, and brushed smoothly from your brow in front, is far more suitable. If I could see your mother I would speak to her on the subject myself.'

'You can't,' said Rosamond. 'She does not live here. The person of the house is my married sister, and she is upstairs, ill.'

'A baby, I suppose?' inquired Mrs Dodman, with stern disapprobation.

'Oh, no!' said Rosamond, with an inward chuckle. (Rica – *Rica* with a baby!) 'Her head aches, and she is very hot.'

'Anything infectious?' the lady inquired, and rose with a little haste from her seat.

Rosamond could not say at present. She volunteered, however, that the children of the house which Mrs Dodman had just left had red spots about their persons and sores on their mouths. 'They *look* catching,' said Rosamond.

The visitor was quickly outside the door. 'Is there anything I can send your sister from the Rectory?' she asked. 'My husband and I consider a labour's wage, *with management,* sufficient to supply the needs of persons in that station. But in times of sickness we are glad to be of assistance.'

'My sister would be glad of a little brandy,' Rosamond said, gazing into the stout lady's heated face with her quick-glancing eyes. 'My brother-in-law, too, would like a drop for a pain he has in the body through working in the sun.'

The clergywoman unsnapped the bag at her waist, and, hastily fumbling amid its contents, produced the leaflets.

'If you will read these,' she said, 'and will get your sister and brother to read them, you will learn something of the painful, the *fatal* effect of that alcohol to which you are all so sadly addicted. A little broth, or some good jelly, I shall, however, have pleasure in sending you if these things are in accordance with the doctor's orders.'

Mrs Chaney, decent woman, curtseyed an invitation to the strange lady to enter. 'Nothing was never lost through being civil,' was a maxim Mrs Chaney impressed in vain upon her ill-conditioned neighbour, and few things were there Mrs Chaney liked better than a half-hour's gossip over the follies and failings of the other labourers' wives. But Mrs Dodman held out her leaflets at arm's length. If she had come to Dulditch for change of air, and should carry home fever, for instance, to her husband and only son!

'I am a little hurried to-day,' she explained. 'If you will read these, please, and pass them on to your friends. They are papers which have had a most convincing effect in my husband's parish.'

As the lady sailed down the little garden path, making an exit as hasty as was consistent with dignity, Rosamond, looking out of her front door, broom in hand, made grotesque salutations to poor Mrs Dodman's back. Reaching the meadow, the retreating visitor turned unexpectedly, and caught the girl in the act. Mrs Dodman stopped, uncertainly gazing, and Rosamond, obeying the impulse of mischief which seized her, scampered down the garden path and leant over the palings.

'I've something to tell you if you'll promise to keep it secret,' Rosamond said. Then dropping her voice very low, but speaking with great distinctness, 'I've–got–a–young–man!' she said.

'Dear me!' said Mrs Dodman, drawing back with rebuking gravity. 'I'm extremely sorry to hear it.'

Rosamond turned and nodded back to the house. 'He lives there with us. He's our lodger,' she said.

'And you seventeen!' said Mrs Dodman, with shocked severity. 'And a hobbledehoy of about the same age, I suppose?'

'He was twenty-six last fourteenth of May,' said Rosamond, delightedly supplying the detail.

'And you and he actually contemplate matrimony?'

'He's never so·much as named the word,' the girl said. 'But as for me, I contemplate it.'

A big blush came rushing to her cheek here, shocking herself as much as her interlocutor.

'In a class of life different from your own,' said Mrs Dodman, severely, 'such notions do not enter the young lady's head until the gentleman puts them there.'

'When he does, you'd think the surprise would kill her,' Rosamond commented.

But she was all at once ashamed of her impulse to play the fool, and without another word went running back to the house again.

CHAPTER TEN

A Female Jack Sheppard

WHEN supper was over that night, the little party seated round the table looked with eyes of surprised alarm at the empty dish upon which the cold joint had made its appearance.

'Not an atom left, and only Monday night!' Rica ejaculated.

'I should hope,' said Eustace, doubtfully, looking across the table to his brother, 'that, becoming accustomed to the conditions of our life, you and I can never be so hungry again as we were this evening.'

Tony raised his eyebrows and shook his head; he was still turning about, with much interest in their anatomy, picking out a morsel of meat here and there, the rib bones on his plate. 'I won't answer for myself,' he said. 'It certainly seemed phenomenal, but we may be destined to exhibit a series of abnormities – one never can tell.'

'It's through everything being so nicely cooked and so beautifully served,' Rosamond said complacently. 'I see I must contrive to have things not so appetising for you.'

'It was unfortunate my feeling well just in time to claim my share,' Rica lamented, whereupon her husband reached forth his hand and clasped hers under the table.

'There was such an unnecessary amount of bone,' Eustace said, looking round with knit eyebrows upon the plates. 'It seems a little hard we should have to pay for all this waste. You must have gone marketing badly, Rosamond.'

'Anyone but Rosamond,' said Tony, 'would have bought the pig's leg instead of his ribs. A good, honest bone running through the middle – and one knows what one has to expect.'

'And there's a cut-and-come-again look about the joint,' Eustace reflected. 'And when you've cut your last, there's still the bone on the dish to remind you of what has been; but –' here he waved his hand eloquently to the empty willow-pattern, and was silent.

'But is there money enough for a pig's leg?' Rica demanded, doubtful-eyed.

'Money? Money and credit too,' said Rosamond, injudiciously; and Eustace, upon whose ears Rosamond's unimportant utterances fell, as a rule, unheeded, unfortunately heard, and pounced upon that word.

'Credit?' he repeated, and his blue, near-sighted eyes were quite alarmingly fierce as they glared upon his sister-in-law through his glasses. 'What do you mean by credit, Rosamond?'

'Why, I meant ready money, of course,' said Rosamond, making a great clatter with the teacups, which she was collecting to wash.

'You understand,' said Eustace, very distinct and impressive, 'I'll have no getting into debt – not for a ha'penny! We're here to make an experiment, not to play the fool.'

'It looks very much to me as if we were doing the two things at once,' said Rosamond, who was angry with herself, and so with all the world.

'A nice hand you've made of it! What are you going to do now?' Tony inquired of her when, later in the evening, she passed him, with her basket in her hand, on her way to Mrs Barrett's.

'What do I care for his threats and his savage looks! I'm not going to let Rica and the children starve, you may be sure,' she said. 'What can he do? He can't kill me. Moreover, he won't know anything about it.'

The husbands on either side of Eustace, their evening meal being over, plodded heavily into their gardens, and having dug and delved mother earth all day, dug and delved her again till the shades of night fell and it was time to turn in for that heavy, dreamless slumber which fitted them for the delving and digging to-morrow. The alternative evening's entertainment was to pass the hours drinking adulterated beer in the kitchen of the White Hart Inn. But one of these was too sober a man to avail himself of this distraction, and the other had too long a score against him chalked up upon the door of the public-house.

There was a small plot of land in the garden which Eustace had promised himself to rid of its dry pea-stalks and to dig for cabbages. But when the opportunity came, he found his flesh so unwilling that for once his spirit's energy was conquered.

Every bone in his body ached, his hands had blistered upon the hoe; on the bridge of his nose and the back of his neck and the outer edges of his ears he got his wife to dredge flour, no other cooling remedy being at hand, and the pain of the blistered skin great. His feet, from standing all day in the hot, dry soil, were tender to a degree. His wife holding tightly to his arm, he limped over the meadow roadway and the scorching meadow grass, and stretched himself beneath a straggling thorn hedge. There he lay, Rica sitting beside him, till the setting sun, having 'drenched with its splendours' all the western sky, and flung its streaming fires high up into the heavens, sank subdued – till over the grassy slope came low, quiet sounds of breezes rustling – till in the sober skies of evening the stars of night appeared – till Rosamond, having lit the shadeless lamp on the kitchen table, called to Rica that the dews were falling, and that it was time for them all to go to bed.

-✂✧✂-

She had returned from her shopping expedition with a crestfallen expression of face, and when Tony inquired of the success of her mission, she showed in her replies that her temper was more than a little ruffled.

'What have you been doing with yourself?' she asked of him; and was informed that he had smoked his pipe in the neighbouring garden, and had watched Nobbs pull up his onions.

'What a fine, intellectual feast!' Rosamond cried derisively.

'It's good to have a feast of some sort,' Tony reminded her. 'Feasts of the intellect, from what you tell me, are likely to be the only ones we shall enjoy.'

It was too true. Rosamond, having gone forth resolved to buy the biggest, most bounteous joint which pork butcher could supply, had met with the discouraging intelligence that the pig who had died on the previous Thursday, the last of his component parts having been long since disposed of, would have no successor to the sacrificial knife before Thursday next.

'Why, if I was to have half a score pigs, miss, who do you suppose would buy 'em?' Mrs Barrett asked of her intending customer. 'None of my customers have the money to buy more than their one bit o' meat, so where'd be the sense in perviding of it?'

And this had not been the worst, for when Rosamond had inquired into the price of some tinned fish which stood on the counter, Mrs

Barrett had unwillingly produced a letter she had just received at the hand of one of the little Nobbs boys. It was signed Eustace Patten, and it set forth his command that on no account was the shopkeeper to supply any of his household with goods for which they did not bring the money to pay.

'So Eustace was too many for you!' Tony said, as he sat, swinging one leg upon the kitchen table, and watching the girl, who had sunk dispiritedly into the chair behind the door. She roused herself sufficiently to fling her empty basket across the kitchen by way of answer. '*That* for Eustace!' she said, at which Tony laughed.

'How I *hate* you!' cried Rosamond, and stamped her foot at him.

'Mary looks so pretty when she's cross,' Tony said reflectively.

Rosamond got up and picked up her basket, and hung it on its peg. 'I wish Mary were here to starve with you instead of me,' she said viciously.

'You ought to be proud of the privilege of starving with me. I thought you would have been.'

'If there'd been at Mrs Barrett's anything to *steal*, I wouldn't starve for fifty Eustaces,' she said.

'And was there really nothing at all?'

'Nothing but this,' she said, and approaching him held up her pocket. 'Tug it out, Tony, it's tinned salmon. I stuffed it in when she wasn't looking. I dared not put it in the basket for fear it should rattle and she should look.'

'You little wicked wretch! You female Jack Sheppard! You gallows bird!'

'Mother will pay her afterwards. Horrid old thing! She might have *given* me something. I showed her the three shillings in my purse, and she said we should want every penny of it for bread.'

Tony with some difficulty dragged out the red-papered tin, flung it to the ceiling, and caught it again. 'Hooray!' he said, 'here are we with a tin of salmon and a loaf or two of bread between ourselves and starvation. Hooray for the Patten Experiment! Lucky for you all I held a certain interesting conversation with our neighbour, the illustrious Mr Nobbs, to-night!'

When the younger Patten came home to dinner next day he, too, had been to the shop. He returned with several little rings of wire in his pocket, which, the meal being over, he showed to Rosamond.

She was in a depressed frame of mind, and, if the truth must be told, a little hungry, as were all the family that day. Rosamond had consulted with Mrs Chaney on the possibilities of the day's dinner, and had produced, at her suggestion, more dumplings, to be eaten with the pork gravy, which, however, at the last moment, was found to have 'gone bad' with the heat, and had to be thrown away. Treacle had, therefore, been substituted, and, in accordance with Eustace's suggestion, a cabbage had been cooked.

'The poor do not make the best use of their materials,' he informed the household. 'There is a nice row of cabbages in the garden. Let us have a cabbage each day for dinner.'

But unfortunately the smell of the cooking cabbage had turned Eustace and his wife so ill that they had no appetite for the rest of the repast; they took each a slice of bread into the meadow to eat, when the air should have restored them.

It was thought that to the children, too, their meal would seem sweeter in the open air. They ate what they could of it, therefore, seated on their little chair and stool in the neighbourhood of the pump, where all the little Nobbses from next door stood around to look at them. Bel, who had a majesty of her own, sent them flying, with the exception of Bay's friend, Josher. His mother had forgotten to supply him with dinner to take to the school that day, and so he had toddled home with the rest, and now shared the delighted Bay's repast, seated on the gravel at her feet. He was attired in a skirt of red and black check, patched in places with bits of blue serge, of which latter material his ridiculous bodice was constructed. This bodice had been his mother's for many years, and still, dwindled as it was, to a large extent retained its original form and fashion. His light hair was scant, and of that kind which no amount of training will induce to lie flat upon the head.

'No one to look at it would think as I dressed his hid with grease ivery day,' his mother said.

His loose, baby mouth hung open, his blue eyes goggled; but, such as he was, he appeared to Bay Boyan a delightful creation, and had almost taken the place with her of the beloved dolly Maude to which she believed she had forfeited all claim.

Rosamond having taken the slight to her dumplings as personal to herself, Tony, left alone with her, dared not refuse a helping. He ate two with valiance, but Rosamond, watching his gulpings down with uneasy eyes, concealed a horrible fear that they might make him ill.

'They're very nice,' he said, in answer to her anxious looks; 'but it isn't everyone that has the digestion for them. If I were you, I'd keep us to bread and cheese, Rosamond. If you wish to vary the menu with a cabbage, cut it up with oil and vinegar and let us have it raw. I can't help thinking such a smell as this is insanitary.'

So poor Rosamond carried the dumplings next door to the Nobbses, whose eyes glistened at the prospect; and with the cabbage chopped up in the yellow basin for the benefit of the chickens, she followed Tony out of doors.

Then he began as he smoked, to manipulate the copper wire, and, she watching his clever-looking fingers with interest the while, he told her he was fashioning snares to catch her father's rabbits.

'Poaching!' Rosamond breathed in a note of deep admiration. 'Oh, Tony, how splendid of you!'

He and Nobbs had had much talk, it appeared – a very intelligent, decent fellow, Nobbs. He had acknowledged, Tony putting it to him artfully, that he and his wife and children did not live by bread alone, but by the judicious annexing, in and out of season, of his master's property.

'And I thought if I could get you a couple of rabbits for the commissariat, Rosamond, I should be doing a good and a useful thing.'

Rosamond gazed upon the hero with approving eyes. 'You are becoming quite a reckless kind of person, aren't you, Tony? A frequenter of public-houses and a poacher!'

'I'm getting on,' Tony admitted, dispassionately.

'Do you know, I like men to be a little wicked, Tony.' She was leaning over his shoulder as she made the admission, and her loose brown hair fell against his cheek. He caught a lock of it in his hand.

'That reminds me,' he said, feeling in his jacket pocket; 'I got these for you. Look!' He produced a box of hairpins. 'It was the outlay of a penny, but it is for the family good. To keep that hair of yours out of the messes – I beg your pardon, the culinary triumphs – for which we are indebted to you.'

'How horrid you are, Tony! And how rude!'

'Rude, my dear girl. One would think, for your own sake, you would prefer to keep your wig to yourself. I have seen you mix it in the dumplings, drop it in the gravy, wash the plates and dishes with it, dip it in the tea.'

'Some people like my hair, anyhow,' said Rosamond, aggrieved, her thoughts flying at once to the admiring Alan Mason.

'I prefer it on your head,' said the unmoved Tony.

She sat by his side in offended silence for some time, while she wove the errant locks into stiff braids, and when that work was completed he, obligingly putting his own task aside, twined the braids with natural dexterity about her shapely head.

'It'll have to keep so till you get a leisure half-hour to fasten it up again,' Rosamond said. 'I can't be expected to waste time over my hair.'

'I'll do it for you every noon-time,' he promised, magnanimously, 'if you remind me.'

Mrs Nobbs, leaning against the post of her front door, was fairly scandalised at what she saw. 'A-takin' their meals and a-doin' of their hair out-doors! 'Tain't like Christian men and women. I never see sech a-goin's on in my life!' said Mrs Nobbs, muttering, yellow-lipped, to herself.

Her own children and the Chaneys and Boyans were calling to each other and running wildly round in a ring on the grass before starting for afternoon school. Josher, silent and unsmiling, tumbled down at every opportunity, but Bay always held him tightly by the hand, and never failed to wipe the dust off his knees and out of his mouth and eyes with her own pocket-handkerchief when she picked him up again.

'I expect I look a perfect fright?' Rosamond inquired, frowning and twisting her head uneasily under its unaccustomed load of hairpins. She glanced with anxiety at Tony, who considered her in a minute's solemn silence, and silently turned back to the manufacture of his snares again.

'Old Eustace won't approve of this, you know,' he said presently. 'The old chap's quite capable of refusing to eat anything that's been poached, if he's starving.'

'We shall have to bamboozle him,' said Rosamond, with calmness. 'It is the fate of the unco' guid to be bamboozled. I'm glad you are not so good as he is, Tony.'

'He's a great deal too good for you, my girl.'

'All the same, I wouldn't have to marry him for all I can see, Tony.'

'But it isn't a question of marrying either of us,' Tony reminded her.

After which Rosamond edged a little away from the young man and was silent.

Presently Nobbs and Chaney appeared at their gates, and Eustace joining them, Tony put his snares in his pockets and went off once more to work.

CHAPTER ELEVEN

Hetherington asks for One

AT tea-time that night it was observed with some consternation that Bel had not returned from school. Bay and her familiar, looking, with his large-pointed ears, his huge head, his upstanding scant hair, more like the popular representation of an imp whose home might be the toad-stool than a little embryo farm-labourer of Dulditch, being dragged from that happy hunting-ground at the end of the Nobbses' garden which was used as a dust-bin by the family, could give no information. Bel had come out of school with the rest but had straightway run off with Ivan Cattle, leaving Bay and the sweet little fellow whom she had made her special charge to come home alone.

Rica was roused to alarm. 'What would mother say, Rosamond? Oh, what a responsibility it all is! I'd no idea that anything could be so thoroughly disagreeable.'

The tin of salmon was opened and its contents divided between the two men. 'Our bread-winners must be thought of first,' the girls said, and both declined the delicacy.

'There is possibly death in the dish,' Tony said when the last morsel had disappeared. 'But one may as well die of ptomaine poisoning as of starvation – a quicker process, perhaps.'

Rosamond hastened to reassure him. 'If you get a good brand tinned things are safe. Mrs Barrett told me so,' she said.

'Tinned!' echoed Eustace. He opened his eyes till his large round glasses were filled with them, glaring accusingly upon Rosamond. 'Was this fish *tinned*, Rosamond?'

'Did you suppose that Rica and I had caught a slice of salmon in the pond?' Rosamond asked with disdain. 'What should it be if it isn't tinned?'

'I should certainly not have eaten it had I known,' he said weightily. 'Darling,' turning to his wife, 'how glad I am you took none of it!'

She regarded him with wide eyes of apprehension. 'Oh, Eustace, you're sure you don't feel ill?' she asked him.

He shook his head, but remained for the rest of the meal eating nothing and ominously silent. Once or twice Rosamond, watching, saw him pass his hand over the region of his stomach with an uneasy look.

'Nonsense, my dear fellow, it wouldn't come on so quickly as that,' Tony said, noting the same action. And then Rica burst into tears.

'If Eustace is ill I shall feel Rosamond is his murderer,' she cried.

'She'll have murdered both of us,' said Tony.

At which point there came a sound of sobbing outside, and a miserable little Bel, with soiled pinafore and scratched and bleeding hands, appeared at the door.

'Oh, Rica! Rica!' she cried, and, hurling herself into the kitchen, flung her little body into her sister's arms. 'They've taken – taken poor Ivan Cattle and put him into prison!'

She shouted the tremendous intelligence amid bursts of sobbing. If she had been proclaiming, Cassandra-like, the destruction of Dulditch she could not have worn a more tragic mien.

When she was in a condition to give a coherent account her family plied her with questions.

Poor Ivan Cattle had just gone into the Rectory garden to secure a few late gooseberries, which he happened to know were growing there, protected from the birds by netting. He hadn't got above a handful, poor little boy! when the gardener, horrid, *horrid* wicked man, came and caught him, and, spite of kicking and shrieking, dragged him away, telling him he should go to prison. He hadn't, however, gone to prison at once, but was shut up somewhere at the Rectory.

Asked how she knew these particulars, Bel confessed that she had been on the spot and witnessed the harrowing scene. Being questioned as to how she came in that locality, she admitted, with a fresh burst of grief, that she also had gone to steal gooseberries, but that Ivan, poor little boy! had been caught while she had run away.

Now, the code of honour by which the young Boyans held was not a particularly severe one. They were not always obedient to their superiors, nor were they invariably respectful to those in authority. Duties staring them plainly in the face they sometimes shirked, and they occasionally permitted themselves the use of the harmless, necessary evasion. But there were two points on which they insisted with relentless firmness: you must not desert your friend in his trouble, and you must never, never run away.

The elder girls, therefore, heard of Bel's performances with great disgust and anger, and when they told her that she had disgraced herself and them, her sobs became redoubled.

It was decreed by the two sisters that she must, as far as possible, repair the wrong she had done the family's sense of decency by going back at once to the Rectory, owning up about the gooseberries, and either procuring Ivan's release or insisting on sharing his punishment. It was further arranged that, as Bel was too cowardly to go on this mission alone, Rosamond should accompany her.

So, all away across the meadow and through the orchard at the back of the farmhouse, and through a couple of fields white for harvest, and down the road which lay between the Cherry-tree Cottages and the

Rectory, Rosamond improved the occasion by telling Bel what she thought of her.

If anyone had told her, Rosamond said, that her little sister Bel had turned murderer or highwayman she might have believed it, and would have received the intelligence with a measure of serenity; but woe be to that person who had ventured to assert in her hearing that the youngest but one of the Boyans had betrayed all the traditions of the family and deserted her companion in guilt!

The reverend gentleman, for whom the girls asked, was out, they were told; and upon their requesting to see Mrs Dodman they were shown into the study. It was a room quite familiar to them, for the relations of Dulditch Rectory and Bunwick Hall were eminently friendly. Rosamond felt the presence of the red-faced, large, untidy-looking wife of the *locum tenens* an intrusion in that quiet, shabby room, sacred to the memories of the gentle, absent-minded rector and his maiden sister.

Mrs Dodman did not invite her visitors to sit down, but eyed them with a suspicious, even hostile gaze, as they stood within the door.

'I have brought my little sister,' Rosamond announced. 'She has something to say to you. Now then, Bel.'

But Bel, quailing before the gaze of the large, stout lady, was dumb.

'A little boy stole some gooseberries from the Rectory garden this afternoon,' Rosamond began.

Mrs Dodman assumed a more upright position in her chair, a great access of colour flew to her red face.

'Gooseberries?' she repeated. 'In my garden? *My* gooseberries?'

Just then a figure appeared at the open window. 'Hetherington,' cried the lady of the heated face, 'come in, dear. Your father never told me we had been robbed this afternoon – robbed of gooseberries. Pray, are you aware of it, Hetherington?'

'Oh, yes!' Hetherington said. 'I have got the thief locked up in the coach-house, and there he is to stay till the governor comes home.'

'These persons have come to give information,' Mrs Dodman explained, indicating the two by the door. And Hetherington, a small and weedy-looking youth, with a ferret face, and his hands in his pockets, glanced, with eyes too close to the bridge of his nose, at the pair.

'This little girl also stole the gooseberries,' Rosamond said. She had told the degraded Bel that she felt humiliated by her errand, but neither her bearing nor the tone of her voice conveyed that impression. 'She has come to apologise, and to ask that the little boy be liberated.'

'But he has not yet been punished,' objected Mrs Dodman. 'I don't know what Mr Dodman's views may be on the subject.'

'He said the thief was to stay in the coach-house till he came home,' said Hetherington, at the window.

'Exactly so. A boy who thieves must be made an example of. And this unhappy little girl–! What is your age, child?'

'I'm seven,' said Bel, who had ceased to cry. She felt not so much fear of Mrs Dodman and her ugly son as hatred of them.

'To be a thief at seven years of age!' said Mrs Dodman, with awful solemnity. She turned and beckoned to her son, who advanced into the room, his particularly ill-becoming bowler hat pushed to the back of his narrow head.

'Take your hat off, Hetherington,' his mother said sharply, and the youth obeyed. 'It seems to me,' she went on, 'if it was your papa's wish to retain one culprit till his return, the other also must be secured.'

Hetherington's white-lashed eyes blinked at Rosamond; he nodded with an air of wisdom very misleading. 'Pa'll want to find them both there when he comes home,' he said.

'As you came to confess your sin, I suppose you came to share the other thief's punishment?' Mrs Dodman inquired of Bel. She really felt it was a grievous sin which the child had committed. To steal just any gooseberries would have been a crime, but the Rectory gooseberries –! Sacrilege! She was quite as shocked as she seemed, and did not for a second doubt that in punishing the offender she was carrying out the will of the Almighty. It may be said that of the wisdom of any course which presented itself to her she never doubted. Mrs Dodman lived and drew her breath in confidence of heavenly applause.

Bel grasped her sister's hand tightly; she knew now how soldiers felt when they stood to die by a fallen comrade. 'I wish to be locked up with poor little Ivan,' she said.

So presently, she still clinging to Rosamond, the stout lady walking on the other side of her lest she should meditate escape, they set out for the coach-house. Hetherington accompanied the procession. He appeared, although so short and narrow, of about nineteen years of age. He walked with an odd, jerky motion, as though his legs were not quite under his control, and he had a trick of alternately shaking and wagging his head, upon the back of which again sat the bowler hat, as if he were continually assuring himself of something – that his head was on his shoulders, perhaps.

'This is the young woman of whom you heard me speaking to papa last night,' his mother told him, as they walked along.

'Oh, yes, yes!' Hetherington said, and his head nodded many times in Rosamond's direction.

'I am glad to find you profited by my advice in one particular,' the lady pursued to the girl, with a kind of restricted approbation. 'The hair worn so is much more becoming – I mean becoming to your station,' she added hastily, lest she should be suspected of meaning a compliment. 'It was hanging loose about her ears,' she explained to her son, who screwed up his lips tightly, as if about to whistle, looked hard at the red-brown knot, beneath Rosamond's sailor hat, and nodded with greater rapidity than ever.

'I hope you have borne in mind the other words of warning and advice I gave you?' Mrs Dodman continued, and Rosamond said, sedately, she remembered every syllable.

'And where, pray, is the young man of whom you told me?'

'He said something about going to try for a rabbit or two,' Rosamond said, unable to deny herself the pleasure of shocking her questioner.

'Poaching!' cried the lady. She stood still on the path, and they all stood still. 'And you can speak of it in that light manner? It was probably he who had the impertinence to set snares to hedges of the glebe? However, Mr Dodman is the right person to deal with that kind of man. Let him look to himself!'

Here Hetherington nodded triumphantly at Rosamond. 'Pa's gone for the police,' he said.

The underfed children of the farm labourer are not a courageous race, and Ivan Cattle's whereabouts might have been known to anyone within a quarter of a mile of the coach-house which held him captive by the dismal howls emanating therefrom. As the little party approached the prison they also distinguished loud sounds of violent kicking upon the door.

'You'll be all right,' Rosamond whispered to her sister; 'there's nothing to be afraid of. Keep quiet and be a brave girl.'

So Bel offered no resistance – seemed, indeed, almost to welcome her fate. 'Ivan! Ivan! I'm coming in too,' she cried, as Ivan, finding the door open, made a dash for liberty.

The Dodmans caught the poor youth and thrust him back, and hastily pushing Bel inside, pulled the great doors to upon both children.

The shooting of bolts, top and bottom, and the falling into place of the big bar which ran across the middle, must have sounded terribly alarming to the prisoners. But Rosamond noted with satisfaction that there was no key in the lock, the bolts and bars being deemed sufficient to protect the seldom-used, shabby old dog-cart, the only vehicle kept by the Rector of Dulditch.

'If you will return with me to the house, I will give you a can of nourishing soup which I have to-day prepared for your sick sister,' Mrs Dodman said to the girl.

But Rosamond declined, and not with thanks. 'My sister does not want any soup,' she said.

'Horribly independent! And how ungrateful!' Mrs Dodman commented, as she walked away with her hand upon her son's shoulder. 'The police papa has gone to fetch must be told about this family. They appear to be quite without principle.'

Hetherington said he expected there would be a lark when pa came home. He nodded confidentially to the grass beneath his feet, screwed up his lips, and drew them tightly in again in a line across his face. Then having dropped his mother at the study window, he walked away, his uncertain legs describing half circles from the knee, or thrown out in front of him with an appearance of jauntiness quite beyond his control, and retraced the steps he had recently taken.

'Are they such fools as to imagine I should let those children remain to be frightened by their policeman?' Rosamond asked of herself as she walked away.

She went out by the way indicated by Mrs Dodman, that is, through the kitchen garden, the scene of poor Bel's undoing, and down the back drive; but having got herself off the premises that way, she proceeded to re-enter them by another, with which she was equally familiar. She cut across the little drying-ground, where she, as a child, had sometimes helped the rector's old housekeeper, cook and general manager, Mary, to catch her chickens in the spring, through the long shrubbery of laurels which screened the stables from the road, and so made her way to the coach-house.

She put her lips to the keyhole, of which, mercifully, the key had been lost. 'Bel,' she whispered, 'I'm here! I'm going to let you and Ivan out.'

'Be very quick, if you please,' Bel called back, her trembling voice nearly lost in Ivan's moans and bellowings, 'the poor boy is so very frightened.'

Rosamond shot back the bolts top and bottom, but the rusted iron bar was more difficult to move than she had expected. She turned away, stooping to pick up a large stone with which to hammer it, when she felt something move between her and the coach-house, and, hastily raising

73

herself, found Hetherington Dodman blinking upon her, and standing up with his back against the barred door.

He was not very tall as yet, but he had lately started growing, perhaps, for his red, flat wrists showed a broad, raw space beneath his coat-sleeves, and there was a good deal of pale-coloured, loose-hanging sock between the bottom of his trousers and his shoes.

He shot out his loose lips at Rosamond, and drew them in across his cheeks, and repeated that trick once or twice before he spoke.

'I thought what your little game would be,' he said at length.

'In all my life I never saw such a Thing to call itself a man,' was all Rosamond, furiously angry at the unlooked-for check, could retort.

'I am one, though,' the youth said, apparently not at all offended. 'I knew you'd come back. I ain't goin' to let you unbar the door till you've given me something.'

'Given you something?' the girl repeated. 'What "something"?'

'Something you give to your young man. Him that's gone poaching in the glebe to-night.'

'As it happens, I give him nothing. Nothing!' Rosamond declared, with red cheeks, emphatically.

'Something he takes, then,' the ferret-eyed youth persisted, and, with a dreadful significance, screwed up the flabby lips.

'You abominable little wretch! Stand away from the door!' Rosamond cried.

He was such a feebly-made thing, she thought easily to move him, but he had planted his back against the door, and stuck his heels in the gravel, and beyond pulling his arm out of his trouser pocket, she did not effect much with all her strength and good-will.

'Give me one, and I'll come away,' the youth said.

Rosamond drew back, panting.

Bel's little voice, tearful now, came through the heavy door.

'Let us out! Let us out, Rosamond! Ivan's so afraid!'

Hetherington, without moving his position, rapped his red knuckles upon the door.

'Policeman'll soon be here!' he croaked.

Thereupon a louder yell arose from the incarcerated Ivan, and once again his iron-toed boots were brought to play, with the energy of despair, upon the door.

With hatred gleaming from her eyes and scorching her cheeks, Rosamond regarded the young man before her. He wagged his head at her, making his odd grimace.

'Over in a minute, you know,' he said encouragingly. 'I shouldn't tell pa or ma.'

In a pause of the noise made by the agitated Ivan, the sound of approaching carriage wheels made itself heard.

'The police,' said Hetherington, confidentially.

'On your honour, you detestable little Beast, would you open the door then?'

'On my honour!'

So Rosamond, advancing a cautious step, held her body well out of his reach and put out her reluctant cheek for his salute.

'Here, then, little Horror,' she said. 'No; not where my dimple is! Here, and be quick!'

It was only a peck that she allowed him, but, as good as his word, he at once turned and unbarred the door, while Rosamond, stooping, plucked a handful of grass, moist with the evening dew, and fiercely rubbed with it the polluted cheek. Which done, she flung the grass, with a vicious aim, in the face of the deliverer, and, with Bel clinging to her skirts, walked away.

Ivan had burst first through the opening door, dashing Bel aside as he did so, and without a word or a look around him, had scampered away home.

CHAPTER TWELVE

Hetherington Receives Payment

THE girls found the cottage empty when they reached home. Mrs Chaney, the ever-at-hand, was however promptly on the scene with the unwelcome intelligence that the pump had 'give out' at last; that there wasn't no longer enough water to be wrung from it to wash a pair of hands; that Mr and Mrs Patten, accompanied by Bay, had, in the emergency, carried a pail across the midder to the well; and that they had promised Mrs Chaney as she should have a kittleful of it for to-morrow's breakfast.

Of Mr Tony, Mrs Chaney knew nothing, except that he had gone out half-an-hour ago with Billy Nobbs from next door. She didn't go to look which way they took; that were none of her business, Mrs Chaney said, mildly bristling. She was a little aggrieved, to tell truth, that the young man's choice should have fallen on the left-hand neighbour for a companion, when her own husband – not much to look at, being only five feet high, and 'won'erful silent,' as his wife acknowledged, but worthy for all that – was available.

'Seein' 's Billy he don't bear a good char'cter, and the master he have discharged him, it weren't becomin' in Mr Tony to have chused him,' Mrs Chaney said to herself.

Rosamond, knuckling the door of the left-hand cottage, hastily inquired of the whereabouts of Mr Nobbs, and learnt that he and Tony had gone off an hour ago in the direction of the White Hart. Mrs Nobbs had no doubt that in that attractive hostelry her husband would still be found.

''Tis where he spend most of his evenin's, 'steads o' comin' home to make hisself comf'table over his own fireside,' she grumbled.

Rosamond cast a hurried glance over the filthy interior; the black and greasy bricks, the broken-down chairs, the remains of the last miserable meal, spread on its disgraceful cloth, still occupying, together with a saucepan, a woman's battered hat, and an indescribable comb brush, the table. Three of the youngest children, seated on the sacking which served for hearthrug, were pulling off their rags of stockings and shirts preparatory to going to bed.

That Nobbs should take refuge in the clean-swept, cheerful inn kitchen, small wonder, Rosamond thought, but that Tony also should have done so on this evening, when it was so important that she should see him, filled the girl with anger.

The little party were returning from the well as Rosamond left Mrs Nobbs's cottage. Rica, it could be seen, was insisting on helping her husband with the pail, the consequence being that at every step some of the precious water splashed upon the ground. Bel ran off with the tale of her adventure to her eldest sister, and Rosamond started in the opposite direction. At the public-house or not, somehow Tony must be stopped from going after the rabbits to-night.

Arrived at the door of the White Hart, by which a dealer's cart or two were standing, and from whence issued loud sounds of coarse laughter and boisterous voices, Rosamond's courage failed her. She dared not go in to face the stupid, half-tipsy owners of the voices, not for any shrinking on her own account, but because she knew that Tony would be angry. She walked once or twice past the inn in an irritable suspense.

'Horrid of him! Why doesn't he come out?' she said.

If she had been shut within prison walls, and Tony, thinking of her, had walked outside, she would have known, she was sure.

She went round to the back of the inn, where the private sitting-room opened on a little garden, in which the wife of the publican was at that moment gathering a basin of broad beans for to-morrow's dinner.

'Will you please go and tell Mr Tony Patten I want him immediately?' the young lady said.

When Tony came out in answer to that summons, he was followed by the roar of ugly laughter with which the message had been received. He slammed the door upon the burst of sound, and joined her in the little square, walled-in garden, where, bordering the potato and bean and onion beds, grew carnations, night stocks, mignonette, making the night air sweet with mingled odours. Tony himself was not laughing, Rosamond noticed, nor did he look particularly pleased.

She told her errand quickly. If he had put snares in the hedges of the glebe, he must not take them to-night. A policeman fetched by the rector was watching.

'The glebe!' Tony said. 'What put it into your head that I should want to steal the old rector's game? It is on your father's rabbits alone I have designs, and that only in order to keep your father's children alive.'

'You needn't be so lofty. I thought you ought to know about the policeman.'

'Stuff about the policeman! And another time, Rosamond, you must really curb your natural desire to see me so far that you don't pursue me to the public-house. Such a course is a little marked, to say the least.'

'It is disgusting of you to be here!'

'I'm here on business.'

'Your business is to hoe daddy's turnips.'

'My business just at the present is to snare your daddy's game. At the moment of your interruption I was engaged with my friend Mr Nobbs in treating your daddy's keeper to unlimited drinks in order to soften his feelings and undermine his principles so far that he may conveniently keep out of the way while we are at work.'

'As if Thurgood was to be bribed!'

'As if Thurgood wasn't!'

He asked how she and Bel had fared at the Rectory, and the history of the children's incarceration and release was given him. A disgusting little pig of a Dodman, who made faces and could not walk straight, had let them out at Rosamond's entreaty, he was told.

'What is that on your face?' he asked, bending closer to examine it in the uncertain light.

'It is nothing.'

'Why do you put up your hand to cover nothing? Come here and let me look.'

He took her chin in his finger and thumb and peered closely at her red-brown cheek. The last floating gossamer of gold and rosy pink, of pale green and amethyst, flung back by sinking sun from distant climes, had faded away; even the sober light of evening was beginning to die. Looking deep into the dark blue of the skies, already a star here and there twinkled into existence. In the warm, still atmosphere, the scent of the carnations, for which the landlord was famed, hung with a heavy sweetness. A voice in the inn kitchen started a song; melody and voice gained by the subduing effect of distance and of shut doors. The innkeeper's wife, having filled her basin with broad beans, retired to prepare them for the morrow.

He held her chin in his hand, an upturned, rounded chin agreeable to hold, and ran the thumb of the hand which held it over her cheek.

'What's it like?' she asked him, looking into his face.

'It's – well, it's not very clean,' he told her. 'Here is a little mud, and there a little green, like grass–'

'I wiped something off with a wisp of grass,' she said, her voice trembling a little over an inclination to laugh.

'And here it is red – crimson – and little white blisters are in the red, and you flinch when I touch it.'

'I burnt something out with a stinging nettle,' she told him. 'When we were children we had a governess we hated; we used to burn out her kisses with stinging nettles. It hurts rather, but you don't feel the kiss afterwards.'

'I should think not.' He let go her chin, and slipped the hand which had held it in his own pocket. 'Who has been kissing you?' he asked.

So, not at all unwillingly, because she always longed to tell him everything if he would only condescend, for his part, to listen, she told of the bargain she had been compelled to make for the liberty of the children.

'The policeman would have been there in another minute. What was I to do? You can't think how I hated it, Tony.'

Tony considered her in silence for a minute. 'It's the effect of having your hair put up. He thought you were a grown-up young woman. As a matter of fact, I expect you enjoyed it very much,' he said.

She gave him an indignant look, and was turning away, but he called her back.

'He was a low little beast; and if you tell me honestly you didn't like it, I'll – forgive you,' he said.

She came back gladly at that, and stood at his side again. 'Come home with me, Tony.'

'"Oh, Tony, dear Tony, come home with me now, the clock from the steeple," etc. I can't, my dear child. Nobbs and I have still to reduce the keeper to amiability.'

'Then take me poaching with you, Tony.'

'Absurd baby!' He put his hand on her shoulder and turned her to the little gate in the garden wall.

'Good-bye, Rosamond.'

'Good-bye, Tony.'

'You aren't a bad little girl, you know.'

'I'm not so dear nor so charming as Mary.'

'But you'll do.'

He held her still for a minute with his hand on her shoulder. 'I was wondering –' he said.

'What?' with soft breathlessness. 'I will tell you if I know, Tony.'

'How long you are going to burn out kisses with stinging nettles?'

'That,' said Rosamond, looking away from him, 'entirely depends on the –'

'Enough,' Tony said. 'On second thoughts, I'd rather not have any of your precocious remarks on the subject. Nobbs will be getting uneasy; run away home, Rosamond.'

Was it possible that any harm could come to him to-night? Rosamond wondered. She stopped upon that thought and looked back when she had left the inn some yards behind her; and at the very instant Tony Patten issued from its portals and walked briskly down the road in a direction opposite to that she had taken – the road which led past the Rectory. Rosamond was filled afresh with foolish terrors. 'Oh, after all, he is going to poach the glebe!' she said.

He was not. He walked briskly along till he came to the Rectory gate, where he turned in, walked up the short drive to the front door, rang the bell, and told the servant who answered it that he wished to speak to young Mr Dodman, but would not detain him a minute.

Hetherington came through the dimly-lighted hall, blinking with his ferret eyes, his hands in his pockets; his legs darted wildly around – there was no mistaking his identity.

'You are Mr Hetherington Dodman?' Tony inquired.

He nodded his head at Tony, and pursed up his lips at him. 'I don't think I know you, though,' he said.

'You insulted a lady this afternoon. I've brought you something in payment,' Tony said, and pulled his hand from his pocket and smartly slapped young Mr Dodman's face.

Hetherington had stuck out his pursed-up lips to the furthest at the moment; his smooth cheek presented quite an inviting tract to the stinging hand.

Having relieved his mind to that extent, Tony walked away again, while Hetherington, his hand to his wounded cheek, turning round, encountered his mother, who, called forth by curiosity to see who Hetherington's visitor could be, was just in time to witness the assault.

'But go after him!' she cried, pointing with an eager hand in the direction taken by the assailant. 'Not you, Hetherington; I forbid you to pursue him. Martha! Caroline!' shrieking to the maids in the kitchen. 'A man has attacked Master Hetherington. Run after him. Don't wait a minute. Capture him. Bring him back.'

But the Rectory servants were a little lukewarm in complying, and Tony had disappeared before they, giggling and holding each other, had started in pursuit.

'I never set eyes on him before,' Hetherington said, shaking his head. He wrung his mouth on one side till the degraded cheek presented a hard and smooth surface, and he felt the marks of Tony's fingers with his own.

'What did the man say?' his parents demanded; and Hetherington, blinking at them, thought he had said something about insulting a young lady.

'And have you insulted a young lady?' his father sternly inquired.

Upon which Hetherington at once replied that he had not even seen one.

'I am sure you have not, my darling,' his mother cried. She examined the outraged cheek, and kissed it.

'I think it was – her, you know – that was here this afternoon – her young man.'

'But why should he make this furious assault on you?' Hetherington's mother asked.

Her son's closed lips stretched themselves in a thin line from ear to ear. 'He couldn't think why,' he said.

'It was doubtless this dangerous fellow who helped the thieves to escape this evening,' Mrs Dodman surmised; and Hetherington concurred in that opinion.

'He was very strong,' he said, still feeling his cheek. 'Very good-looking young man, very strong.'

He was not a very brilliant specimen of young manhood himself. Indeed, in spite of untiring efforts of father, mother and tutors, it had been found impossible to impart more than the rudiments of education to Hetherington. He was almost entirely lacking in the moral sense, and Mrs Dodman knew she must never let him out of her sight; but at least he bore no malice, and he had a spirit generous enough to feel admiration. Many times during the evening he spoke in tones of awe of the beauty and the strength of the man who had chastised him.

Between his father and mother it was agreed that their wrongs at the hands of the family at the Cherry-tree Cottages must be redressed, and that Mr Dodman should take early steps to acquaint the owner of the soil on which they lived and worked with the character of the people he was harbouring.

-⚬❈⚬-

Perhaps it was only his imagination that affected him, and the feeling that, having eaten tinned salmon, he ought to be ill – for Tony, who had shared the delicacy, made no complaint – which gave Eustace that alarming pain in the body, keeping his wife and Rosamond anxious far into the night.

Rica, sitting by the sufferer's bedside, applied to the affected part a constant succession of cloths rung out of boiling water, and Rosamond, in the kitchen, kept the kettle boiling with difficulty. The elder sister, in the beginning, was hardly on speaking terms with the younger, supposed to be the cause of the clergyman's suffering, but as his sorrows increased, the need of unburdening herself of her fears pressed too hard upon the wife to be withstood. As they wrung out the cloths for the sixth time, –

'His agonies are unspeakable,' Rica said. 'He tries not to let me see how he suffers, but I know they are unspeakable.'

'Then he must certainly have the doctor,' Rosamond said.

But Eustace overheard this last remark from his bedroom and cried out an emphatic, 'No! No! We can't afford a doctor. We should have to get an order. The relieving officer lives four miles in one direction, the doctor six in the opposite direction. It would be morning before we got him here. I shall be dead or cured by the morning.'

It was Mrs Chaney who had obliged with those particulars in the first stages of Eustace's illness earlier in the evening. She had told how, when she was attacked last harvest-time with the heart's disease, having fainted as soon as she arose in the morning, and her husband not knowing how to keep life in her, it was six o'clock at night before the doctor could come to her assistance. And how, having no one to send for medicine until the next evening, when her husband finished work, it was thirty-six hours before remedies could be got for her, she lying, according to her own account, at death's door all the while.

These facts having made a deep impression on the Reverend Eustace, he was firm in persisting that as he was for the nonce in the position of Mrs Chaney and the rest, he would only seek medical aid under conditions possible to them.

'All the same,' said Rosamond to herself, 'if he isn't better when Tony comes home, a doctor he shall have if Tony has to drag him here by the hair of his head!'

When Rica next made her appearance she was crying; sinking into the nearest chair she put her face down into her hands and tried to smother her sobs.

Rosamond, casting a frightened glance at her sister, flew up the steep, hollow-sounding stairs, and peeped round the open door upon her prostrate brother-in-law. Then she clattered down again and shook Rica by the shoulder.

'The man's not dead!' she said reassuringly. 'I thought at the very least your husband was dead, Rica.'

Rica clung to the younger girl. 'His feet are turning cold,' she sobbed. 'Oh, I happened to feel them, and I know it's a bad sign. I know they don't last long when their feet turn cold. His are cold as ice, Rosamond.'

'Let's "clap a hot brick" to them. It was what Mrs Chaney advised in the first instance,' Rosamond reminded her. 'We ought not to have forgotten about the brick.'

She was groping in the warm darkness of the outhouse, where she remembered to have seen some loose bricks, when she heard the whisper of voices – Tony's voice and that of Billy Nobbs – close at hand. As she gladly called out to them, Nobbs disappeared into his cottage and Tony came forward.

'Are you all right?' she demanded, peering anxious-eyed at him in the darkness. 'Your voices sounded so horribly *secret*, they frightened me.'

'Why aren't you in bed?' he asked her. 'Above all, why are you poking about in the outhouse at midnight?'

She was looking for a brick, she told him.

'Absurd to think of beginning to build at this time of night!' he said, and took her hand and led her in.

'Where are the rabbits and the hares?' she asked him.

He shook his head sadly. 'Alas! Alas! and alas!' he said.

Her disappointment was great, and she reproached him fiercely. To go out poaching – to take that sin upon his shoulders – and to bring home nothing! In that particular line, then, he had proved himself a failure, and Rosamond hated him to fail at anything.

He did not defend himself from her anger, but exhibited a strange docility; he seemed, indeed, to have no excuses to offer. 'I suppose there's nothing to eat?' he asked, and Rosamond said he could have a slice of bread, which he declined.

'You've got to go up and look at Eustace,' the girl, still aggrieved, informed him. 'I don't myself think there's anything the matter with him, but Rica thinks he's dying. If so, and you don't wish for a coroner's inquest, you'd better go for the doctor.'

'And where's the doctor, pray?'

'Only six miles off. To save a dying brother!'

'Dying fiddlesticks! I'm about dead beat as it is. I'll see Eustace at Jericho first.'

'It's only what the other men have to do after their day's work if anyone belonging to them is ill. Go and look at him first, however.'

Eustace had ceased to groan, had refused further hot towels, and was on the point of dozing off.

'Right as rain!' Tony said, returning from the inspection. 'A little brandy would have put him all right from the first.

'Don't say it!' cried Rosamond, and stamped her foot at him. She had heard that phrase about the unprocurable brandy so often.

'You look tired,' he said, considering her with his new strange air of gentleness. 'I have never seen you look tired before.'

'It has been such a fag to keep up the fire with sticks, and I dared not use the coal. But I didn't want to go to bed till you were safe home, and it is well to have something to do. I'm disgusted with you, and disappointed, but I'm glad you're not murdered or anything. Good-night, Tony.'

'No. Sit here, look, in this chair, and I will make you a cup of tea first. It will be a change for one of us to do something for you.'

So Rosamond, very tired, but all at once supremely happy, sat in Nurse Brunton's one arm-chair, while he found another handful of sticks to set the fire sputtering and crackling again, and brewed her a pot of tea. Very smoky was the beverage, and the flavour of Mrs Barrett's one-and-tenpenny prime Indian was not of the best, but Rosamond, who had never in her life before been waited on by Tony, thought the drink which he offered her ambrosial.

There was something of a delicate excitement, too, delightful, never felt before, in sitting there alone with Tony, Darby and Joan fashion, over the embers of the fire – they two the only waking people in the house.

'You must be pretty well sick of this,' he said to her. 'You'll be glad when this mad freak of Eustace's is a thing of the past.'

Rosamond began to declare she had had enough of it, but stopped, being not quite sure she would be altogether glad. 'When it's quite a long way off, Tony, I expect we shall think we were very jolly,' she said wistfully. 'If only there were enough to eat it would not be so very bad even now.'

'You aren't hungry?'

'Oh, if women are hungry or no – what does it matter? But it haunts me in my dreams that there is no dinner for you and Eustace to-morrow.'

'You know, I think you were cut out for a poor man's wife.'

'No, thank you!'

'I don't mean Cherry-tree Cottage poverty – more of the genteel order –'

'No, *thank* you!'

'You've got pluck and resource and selflessness, you know –'

She flushed to her heavy hair with pleasure. 'Come to that, I don't want to be rich,' she said softly. 'I wouldn't be afraid. If I loved him and he loved me, I'd rather scrub floors for him than ride in a rich man's carriage.'

'Even if you loved the rich man?' he inquired illogically.

'Ah, but I sha'n't,' said Rosamond, confidently, with a shy smile.

The appointment which Tony had just obtained as tutor in one of the public schools was to bring him in a hundred and fifty a year. It would not have been well-mannered, Rosamond considered, to show herself contemptuous of poverty!

'On the whole,' said Tony, reflectively, 'you're rather a nice little thing, Rosamond.'

'Oh!'

'You're not free from faults –'

'How *rude* of you!'

'Dear, you're full of 'em, aren't you, now? Come, own up; aren't you full of faults?'

'Yes, thank God!' said Rosamond, hardily.

'To begin with, you have a mighty high opinion of yourself –'

'Go on, pray.'

'A boundless impatience of restraint –'

'Oh, thank you! But I can't sit here till morning while you pelt me with random accusations. You can make out your list to your own satisfaction. I am going to bed.'

He called to her as she passed up the stairs, 'Don't bother about the empty state of our insides, dear. I'm going to get something for the pot to-morrow, or perish in the attempt.'

'Nonsense! You must go to work. I won't have daddy say you shirked your work.'

'Not to-morrow. I have an engagement for to-morrow, and shall take a half-day off.'

CHAPTER THIRTEEN

Tony is 'Wanted'

EUSTACE, looking very seedy from his last night's illness, stooping from the remembered pain, limping on tender feet, but attentive as ever to 'the potent, felt, interior command,' went off alone at half-past five to his labours, leaving Rica, who had had a disturbed night, sleeping in bed. Rosamond and the children had their breakfast alone that morning – a breakfast of dry bread or of bread and treacle as the fancy dictated; but by the time the little ones were ready to start with the small allies from either cottage, Tony Patten was among them. He carried over his shoulder a gun, and in his hand dangled three fine rabbits. Having failed at the snaring last night, Tony had borrowed Nobbs's gun, and the children gave a shout of delight when they saw the 'bag.'

'I'd as soon eat cat as rabbit as a rule,' Rosamond said, 'but to-day I really feel inclined to begin on them before they are cooked. But you, Tony, must pull off their fur coats, and do all the other horrid things to them, please.'

'One is for Nobbs in payment for the loan of the gun,' Tony said.

He was not expert at skinning rabbits. His shirt sleeves were turned up, and he was incarnadined to the elbow, when the posse of children rushing off to the morning school rushed back with the intelligence that a policeman was coming across the meadow.

Bel Boyan's pretty face was white, and her eyes held alarm. She went and stood by Rosamond's side, and grasped her frock. The elder girl put her arm about her, and glanced uneasily at Tony.

'Those horrid Dodmans have sent him,' she said.

Whereat Bay Boyan, dancing on agitated feet, began loudly to proclaim to the four winds of heaven that poor, dear, darling Bel had to go to 'plison.'

Two of the younger, white-haired Nobbses joined artlessly in the lamentation, the older ones looking on with malicious enjoyment.

'Yer shou'n't ha' gone along o' Ivan to steal the guseberries,' they reminded their school companion. Bel, who had been disposed to cry, looked at them proudly with a tightly-held lip.

'Be off!' Tony cried, and waved his ensanguined arms; and at that very moment the policeman appeared in the doorway.

'Good morning! Hope you're not feeling any the worse for that crack of the skull you *would* have last night?' Tony inquired politely of the solid, stolid-looking officer staring at him with dropped mouth and unspeculative eyes.

Tony turned to Rosamond.

'The fact is, you behold in me a captive,' he explained. 'This too-zealous officer interrupted me last night in my laudable attempt to obtain food for to-day's dinner. We came to very high words; indeed, he being indiscreet enough to attempt to handle me, we even came to blows, which, as he had the worst of it, I now deeply regret.'

'This ain't the place for no disclaimers,' the policeman said. 'You can say what you have got to say to the magistrate. Our nearest one, Mr Boyan, being out, you'll come wi' me, a matter o' five miles, to our next. You having showed wi'lence, a brother officer is a-goin' to help me conwey you there in the cart, which is a-waitin' 'crost the midder on the road. There ain't no call for no self-incrumbinations. Take my advice, and come along o' me, quiet.'

'You stupid, impertinent idiot,' Rosamond began, fiercely apostrophising the policeman, 'how dare you speak in that tone to –?'

But Tony gently put her on one side. 'Hsh! Nonsense, my dear child,' he said. 'The man has got to do his duty. It won't be a hanging matter –'

At this unlucky speech, Bay, whose fortitude had been tried to the utmost, uttered a dismal yell, in which the younger and more sympathetic Nobbses loudly joined. In the midst of the uproar, Rica, hurriedly wrapped in her clothes, her hair still unbound, came creeping down the stairs. She pushed open the door of the staircase.

'What *is* going on down here?' she inquired in terrified accents.

The younger child made a rush at her. 'Oh, Rica, Rica! He's going to be hanged,' she cried.

And poor Rica, looking from the startled faces of the little group to Tony, standing with blood dripping from his fingers and the policeman at his side, uttered a loud scream, and threw herself back upon the stairs.

Rosamond, wrought upon by the screaming to an unbearable degree, seized her sister by the shoulder, and shook her unfeelingly. 'The blood on his hands is from skinning a rabbit,' she cried. Whereupon Rica's wild shrieking turned to laughter equally wild, and the poor girl lay on the stairs a victim to violent hysterics.

'That hinformation,' said the policeman to Tony with heavy self-complacency, 'will be used against you.'

'All right, old man,' said Tony, 'do your worst.'

He washed his hands and arms in the basin Rosamond held for him, and pulled down his shirt sleeves. She fetched his red and black striped flannel jacket, and as he slipped in his arms, –

'It's to that empty-headed pompous old Crossway he will take you,' she whispered. 'Daddy hates him, and always quarrels with him on the bench. But he will see you are a gentleman; it will be all right. Only, Tony, don't let it get in the newspapers. Daddy would be so cross.'

The policeman turned a fishy eye upon the children, now huddled together in the doorway, affrightedly looking on.

'Hany of you youngsters hacquainted with a gal and boy what have forced a hentry into the Rectory garden, and have stole the guseberries?' he demanded.

There was an awful silence. Even Rica seemed to stop her distraught laughter to listen. The children heard only their own heartbeats for what seemed to them an age. Then the eldest Nobbs, pointing with a grimy finger at Bel, pronounced, –

'She done it, please, sir. Her and Ivan Cattle.'

The policeman breathed heavily, regarding the culprit. ''Tis the Reverend's wish that you and your accomplish should be dealt with summary,' he said. 'He and me have interviewed the schoolmistress. You and Cattle will be dealt with summary.'

Rosamond did not hear this perplexing announcement. She had Tony by the arm, and was whispering to him, 'Tell the numbskull Crossway that you were father's guest and were shooting his game,' she said.

'That would have been so easy,' he whispered back, 'but unfortunately, dear, I was not sufficiently acquainted with the limits of your father's estate; and it seems it was on old Pettifer's land we snared the rabbits.'

Rosamond gave a groan of dismay, and shook the arm she held. 'How could you!' she whispered. 'He and daddy are the deadliest enemies. He will be delighted; and daddy will never forgive you.'

'These animosities of your daddy's are a little unfortunate under the circumstances,' Tony said. 'But cheer up, Rosamond, you'll have a good dinner at any rate; and, if the Fates are kind, I'll get home to share it with you.'

He cast hungry eyes in the direction of the three skinned rabbits lying in their gore on the table, and he then discovered that the policeman, with a piece of string drawn from his pocket, was knotting the grinning, blood-stained heads together.

'I takes charge of this here walable hevidence,' he said.

And so, with breaking hearts, they had to look on while their dinner was taken from them.

It was not in Rosamond to look on patiently. Converted for the time being into a little fury, she said some very strong things to the policeman, who passed out in his impenetrable armour of stupidity, unscathed by the lightning of her eye, and impervious to the venom of her tongue.

She turned on the children when policeman and prisoner had departed. She thought Bel and Bay were crying so bitterly for the loss of Tony and the rabbits, and she drove them away with angry words, seeking no further explanation of their sobs and their terrified looks.

<hr/>

'I'm glad *I* didn't go after no guseberries!' the eldest Nobbs said as they all ran along.

The little Boyan girls cried as they ran, their heads thrown back; the warm air drove their sobs into their throats until they choked in their grief.

What being punished 'summary' meant they knew not, and were the more frightened at the vagueness of their alarms. Tony in the hands of the policeman, Bel also an offender against the law, and about to undergo an unknown penalty – into what a world of terror and suffering had they not unexpectedly tumbled? – they who had been so guarded and safe and warm. After such a disaster and disgrace no hideous thing seemed impossible. They were set out on a limitless career of unhappiness – mother and home, and their cosy beds and Dolly Maude for ever lost.

Bel was upheld in her anguish to some extent by the thought of Ivan. What she suffered he would suffer likewise. The companionship of guilt had been fatally attractive; even the companionship of suffering had its charm.

But Ivan, as ill luck would have it, was not at school that morning; his little sister arose in her place to make his excuse when names were called.

'If you please, Gov'ness, Ivan's sick. He've got a rash on him, and mother think he's best at home.'

'Yes; and you're best there too,' Gov'ness said sharply. 'Does your mother think because Ivan's got a rash we all want to have it? Go you back home, and stop there till we know what's up with Ivan.'

The child turned her legs over the form, got up, and began unwillingly to walk away. Not one of the children but preferred a day in school to a day occupied in helping mother at home.

'Stay!' said Gov'ness, and the child stopped, while Gov'ness's bright eyes roved slowly over the rows of boys and girls looking up at her. 'Stand!' she commanded, and with a clattering of heavily-shod feet the school arose. They knew that impressive pause before Gov'ness addressed them – they trusted her, and were awed but not afraid.

'There is among you boys and girls,' Gov'ness began, 'a boy and a girl naughty enough to have gone to the Rectory garden yesterday and stolen some gooseberries.'

'Please, Gov'ness,' began the eldest Nobbs, with an eager hand held up to ask attention, 'that were –'

'Silence, Dan Nobbs,' Gov'ness commanded sharply, and brought a book down with a sounding slam upon the desk. 'You dare interrupt me again and you shall be punished with the others!'

It seemed to Bel, in her little muddled brain, that the book had fallen upon the name which had been on Dan's lips, that it was there beneath it, imprisoned on Gov'ness's desk, and might, when the book was lifted, escape and proclaim itself aloud.

'This afternoon,' the alert-looking little woman at the desk went on, her bright eyes moving slowly along the rows of attentive faces, 'the clergyman and the police are coming here, when the naughty boy and girl who did that wrong and foolish thing will be punished in the view of the whole school. I have given you this warning in order that you may let nothing but illness keep you from school this afternoon.'

She paused upon that. 'Now, if they've got any sense, those that did it will be ill and stay away,' said Gov'ness to herself. 'I'm not going to have any whippings in my school that I don't do myself, nor any

89

interference of any Reverend Dodman, who had better go back and manage his own parish, to my thinking.'

'Gwendolen Cattle, go home to your mother!' The child's heavy boots conveyed her noisily to the door.

'Sit!' said Gov'ness, and at the word the rows of boys and girls sank into their places again.

Bel was stupid at her lessons that morning – very hot and tired, and heavy of head. She kept thinking of poor Ivan ill in bed with a rash – what was a rash? – and of her mother – the comfortable, dear mother – and of what she would say if she knew the fright her poor little girl was in. And from this she fell to thinking of Ivan's mother, and wondering if she was large and warm and endlessly comfortable like her own, and had that kind hand, not slight and crushable like Rica's, nor strong and restless like Rosamond's, but firm and gentle and helpful, made for the holding little girls' hands, and for making them feel, while it held them, that they could never, never be afraid.

And soon, in a curious jumble of her confused little mind, she had mixed up her own mother with Ivan's mother, and herself with him, till she thought it was she herself who was ill. Then her head fell on the copy she was making, and she was uneasily asleep.

Gov'ness, finding her so, gently awoke her, looked at child's flushed face and misty, heavy eyes, and sent her home.

'You must have caught cold,' said Gov'ness. 'Run home, my dear, and don't come again till you are well.'

CHAPTER FOURTEEN

A Shock to the System

THAT day was to be an eventful one at the Dulditch parish school.

At twelve o'clock, lessons being over and the children dismissed, those of them at a distance from home repaired to the faggot-stack in the schoolyard to discuss the slice of bread and dripping, bread and treacle, bread and jam with which each had come provided. Then it was that a loud wail arose from Theodora Dack, and on inquiry, it was discovered that her dinner-bag had been robbed.

She was an only child, better off and better fed than the rest; she wore a frill of white lace at throat and wrists, a string of blue beads round her neck, and in her dinner-bag, when she had left it, lay a lump of cake, as well as slices of bread and cheese.

Theodora, now missing the cake, howled with persistence and entire lack of restraint, and wild accusations were shrilled among the little throng about the faggot-stack, each small boy and girl remorselessly charging his and her neighbour with the crime.

In the midst of the tumult the youngest Nobbs, placidly ramming his bread-and-scrape into his huge mouth, was silent, and Bay, who had begged of Rosamond to take her own piece of bread to school that day in order that she might enjoy with Joshua the delights of the *al fresco* feast, listened to the clamour without appetite for her own meal, and with a frightened face, while she held Joshua closely by her side.

For, having been let out with the infant class for half an hour's play at eleven o'clock, it happened that she had missed Joshua from his faithful attendance. Going to seek him, she had met him coming from the direction of the passage where the dinner-bags were stacked, a slice of currant cake in his guilty little paw.

He seemed quite oblivious of this incident now, and his pale eyes goggled from his head in their usual unspeculative fashion. He broke his bread with his claw-like little hands, and stuffed his mouth, as was his pretty custom at meals, breathing stertorously through his mouthfuls the while, being possessed of a nose through which Joshua had never breathed freely since his birth.

There was such a hooting and accusing in shrill, thin voices, such a prolonged and determined bellowing from Theodora, that it brought Gov'ness away from her own dinner she was sharing with husband and children.

'A thief among us! Why, what are we coming to?' she cried, when she heard the story. Her bright eyes, not untroubled, travelled over the eager, now silent, little crowd. She knew that many of them were hungry still though dinner-bags were empty. Often and often she fed the hungriest herself, and in her quick, alert way – O woman of blessed memory! – was always wise and pitiful and kind.

Her eyes paused upon the eldest Nobbs. He was a big boy, a nuisance in the school, of an age to be of use to the farmer, generally badly off for boys, and to be bringing into the miserable family store a good three and sixpence a week; but he was backward in his standards, and hopelessly stupid at his lessons, and Gov'ness knew there was no hope of being relieved of him yet. He had finished his own dinner, but, with a very unsatisfied look in his prominent eyes, was gazing upon a luckless child whose meal was still in progress. He seemed by no means ill at ease, but Gov'ness had her doubts of Dan Nobbs. The boy turned, feeling her eyes upon him.

'He that did the deed had better own up and take his punishment quietly,' Gov'ness said.

'Please, Gov'ness, I see my little brother Josher have a curran', time back,' Dan said quickly, with a happy flash of recollection.

He handed over his fraternal flesh and blood to judgment without a pang. There is not much *esprit de corps* to be found in the village schoolroom. Moral as well as physical courage are both conspicuously lacking. To save your own skin! The son of the country labourer does not go beyond the first and most important of all duties – his duty to himself.

'Joshua would never be so wicked, for sure!' Gov'ness said.

She looked at Joshua, stolidly stuffing in with the palm of his grimy little hand the last fragment of his bread-and-scrape. Bay Boyan, her frightened little face quivering and on the verge of tears, had thrown a shielding arm around the lesser child. Gov'ness, with a tossed head of perplexity, turned her back on the pair and returned to her own dinner.

'S'pose he did steal it, who can wonder? Who's to blame?' she asked of her home circle.

Left to themselves, the children sprang down the faggot-stack and gathered round Joshua and his protectress where they sat on the gravel apart.

'What ye done wi' th' cake?' 'Ah, greedy pig!' 'Who's a thief?' 'Who di'n't keep's hands from pickin' and stealin'?' resounded on all sides.

Josher, almost choked in Bay's embrace, gazed with unmoved countenance at his accusers and said nothing.

Then Dan, pushing his way through the little crowd, smacked the child's white and flabby face with his greasy cap. 'Ugh! Greedy!' he cried. 'To ate it all yourself, and never to give so much as a curran' away!'

⁓⋇⟨⋄⟩⋇⁓

'You did take that cake, didn't you, poor little boy?' Bay inquired of the child when at last the others had run off to the playground and he and she were left alone. She went on her knees as she held him and looked up in his ugly, unwholesome little face with eyes full of love. 'You did take Theodora's cake from the bag, Josher?'

Josher nodded solemnly. 'Curran's in it,' he said heavily.

'But Josher mustn't steal else God won't love him,' Bay assured him. 'I can love Josher still 'cause I'm only a little girl, but God can't love him. You wouldn't like to be a poor little boy that God didn't love, would you, Josher?'

He was only four, and still, as has been said, in petticoats, very small for his age, except in his head, which was abnormal. He had been accustomed, all his life, to take food when he could get it, and he was quite unimpressed by the wickedness of his conduct now. He did not, in the least, comprehend why God did not love him – not that he had any yearnings for spiritual approbation; his stomach, little pot-bellied receptacle as it was, yearned to be full, and that was about the limit of his desires.

Bay Boyan was not impatient of his lack of understanding any more than when she talked to her doll without response. She had always to supply the deficiency of reasoning power in Dolly Maude, and to put words into her mouth, and she quite happily pursued the same course with her later *protégé*.

'If God don't love poor little Josher, poor little Josher won't go to heaven. "Josher wants to go to heaven?" Yes, but he'll see other little girls and boys going there, and he'll have to stay outside. "Let me come in," says Josher; but they won't let you in!'

At that, in a quite unpremeditated way, Josher lifted up his voice and wept. It brought back to his mind an incident of the earlier summer, when he had watched his brothers and sisters going off to the school treat in the Rectory garden meadow, to the enjoyment of tea and unlimited bread and butter and buns, while he, owing to the fact that he was not yet of due age to attend school, had been left at home with his mother.

'I wants to go to heaven!' he howled. 'I wants to go!'

Whereupon Bay became as lavish of her promises as any priest at a death-bed. With the skirt of his dirty frock she wiped his tears away, and sitting down under a hedge with him, cosseted him in her own fat arms. She was only two years older than Joshua, but she had to protect him, she knew. She had to see that he came in the clutches of no policeman, to be haled to prison like poor Tony, or to be birched. And Bay herself wanted to get away from a horrid school, where boys and girls told tales, told lies, exulted in the downfall of their friends, were rude and rough and stupid – not like the boys and girls of her life at all.

So, turning their backs on the children, who were Joshua's enemies and hers, who, their meal done, were now shouting, in voices hoarse or shrill, at their play, she led the child away.

⁘⬦⁘

Bel, released from school, felt better when she got into the open air. She was so unused to illness that she did not recognise its symptoms, felt only an impatience at the heaviness of her head. It was swelled from crying, she thought, and she ran along in the full expectation of getting back to her normal state of feeling soon.

Instead of bending her steps towards the Cherry-tree Cottages, she ran into the village street, and stopped at that cottage by the White Hart where Ivan Cattle lived. She wished to consult with her dear partner in guilt as to what steps she should take to avoid the 'summary' punishment in store for her that afternoon. She had, besides, a penknife in her pocket, which he had coveted and she had denied him, it being the favourite of all her possessions, but to Ivan ill nothing must be refused.

The sun – 'the splendid, silent sun' – was a torture that day to Eustace at his turnip-hoeing. He kept on doggedly at his work, resisting the advice of the seasoned men who worked beside him that he should give up and retire into the shade.

'What you fellows can do I can do,' he said, having a spiritual strength far in excess of his physical power.

When at last he dropped his hoe to walk home in the raging noon, the men noticed pityingly that he staggered in his walk. 'Hold up, master,' one of them said kindly, and put a rough, guiding hand upon his shoulder, 'you and we's made o' diff'rent stuff, I take it. You ain't no more fit to do our wark than we are to do yours.'

Sunk upon the chair within the cottage door, great black shadows floated before his eyes, and he could not even see his wife's face.

She bathed his swelled hands, scorched to painfulness, and his sun-baked, stiff face, with lukewarm water. She would have pulled off his boots and bathed his feet but for the certainty he felt that, once off, his boots would never go on again. Under such ministrations he revived and ate more heartily of the potatoes and the bread and cheese, the only fare which could be put before him, than was good for him, after which a violent pain seized him once more in the chest.

'Of course he has a frightfully bad digestion,' Rosamond declared.

Rica repudiated the notion as haughtily as if it had been an indictment of her husband's manhood. 'If he'd eaten a quantity of rich food you might say so!' she cried; 'but bread and cheese and potatoes – one can hardly have anything plainer to digest, I should think.'

'Whatever he ails, he is not strong enough for this tomfoolery,' Rosamond persisted; 'and you are not strong enough. Tony and I and the children will struggle through, perhaps, but you'll both be on a sick-bed in the finish.'

'For fifty sick-beds, Eustace, having put his hand to the plough, will not look back; and I think you most horribly unfeeling and – and unlike a sister-in-law,' Rica said with a trembling voice.

And Eustace stopped his agonised rockings to and fro to cast fierce darts of anger from his eyes at Rosamond.

''Tis the 'taters,' Mrs Chaney said, arriving on the scene, as she did in and out of season, without the preliminary of knocking at the door. 'He've overloaded his stomich wi' 'taters, and they set won'erful heavy. You han't sech a thing as a spoonful of brandy handy?'

Rosamond turned swiftly on her heel by way of answer, and the good woman, retiring, returned presently with a glass of hot water in which carbonate of soda had been dissolved – a nauseous potion, which Eustace swallowed with the readiness with which he accepted all the disagreeable doses life held out to him.

By the time that his neighbours were seen to be slouching off to their work, Eustace was so far recovered that he insisted on going too. Rica accompanied him. She could not turn her back and leave him toiling in the fields, but sat herself down beneath the poor shade of a close-clipped thorn hedge, from whence she could watch his labours. She had put a cabbage leaf into his hat, and had sewed a large white handkerchief there too, to fall over the back of his blistered neck. Yet, in spite of these precautions, she anxiously expected sunstroke, and was determined to be on the spot.

They had dreaded the effect on Eustace of the story of Tony's exploit, which had to be explained to him. He was too much engaged with his own sufferings, perhaps, to be aroused to agitation over any extraneous matter, for he took it very quietly.

'Tony is always eager for the pleasures of the table,' he said; 'but all experience is useful. He will now see what it is like to be taken as a poacher before the magistrates.'

It was not till late in the afternoon that Tony arrived home. He came in the best of spirits, having taken the precaution to get a good meal at an inn on the way.

'Only eggs, fried with some salt bacon,' he explained, 'but, gracious powers! how I ate! How many eggs do you think I polished off, Rosamond? Ten.'

'Ah, greedy pig!' said Rosamond.

'Wait! In the midst of that high festival did I forget you? Look! The pockets of my jacket are full of eggs – ten in each pocket. When I'd packed 'em in I found I couldn't walk in the jacket, so, for your sake, have had to pad the hoof in my shirt.'

He hung the jacket carefully over the back of the fireside chair, and, followed by Rosamond, took his pipe abroad to smoke it under the ash tree at Mrs Nobbs's corner, where was his favourite retreat. Here, when the desire for speech fell upon him, he related as much as he wished of what had befallen.

'I've got to go before the magistrates at Ornwich on Monday,' he announced. 'You see, it was a pity I hit that poor old buffer over the head last night, but he would have it. However, I daresay it will be all right.'

'Did you tell Mr Crossways who you were?'

'I told him my name and that I was staying at the Cherry-tree Cottages. I didn't go into further particulars for fear of spoiling the lark.'

'The lark won't be so agreeable if you finish the rest of your holiday in prison.'

'The old boy – Crossways – was as stiff as a poker. He kept an alarmed eye on me and evidently thinks me a dangerous character. It was well for young men to come into the country to enjoy its freedom and its pleasantness, he said, but they must learn that to snare the farmers' rabbits and to poach the squire's hares was not permissible.'

'To say nothing of murdering the village constable! Oh, Tony, how angry daddy will be with you!'

'What do you suppose he will do to me?'

'He might tell mother he would not have you asked down again. But you'll come all the same, won't you, Tony?'

Tony would not pledge himself to that, but smoked in silence.

'Wherever else you went there would not be Mary, you know,' she reminded him.

'Oh, rot about Mary!' Tony said, and Rosamond did not resent the remark. She looked in a blissful silence at the meadow rolling away from her feet, 'the Liliput countless armies of the grass' laved in the yellow gold of the afternoon sun; overhead the measureless blue of the sky.

'Ah, how lovely everything is, Tony!' she said, sighing from the fulness of her content. 'I should think, however poor one was, one could not help being happy sometimes in such a beautiful, beautiful world. Just for the privilege of living in the sun and drinking in the air everyone must be grateful.'

'There was a poor devil of a tramp I met just now as I passed through the village. He was shaking with weakness, hunger was stamped on his face; he looked as if no roof had sheltered him for weeks. The sweet

96

influences of sun and air had done nothing for the man that the callousness of men had brutalised. I had a shilling left in my pocket, but, at the first word I spoke, he took fright and slunk off, cursing me as he went.'

'It's a pity to remember these sad things in such a beautiful world, Tony.'

'The pity is when we forget them, Rosamond.'

'Ah! Now you sound like Eustace.'

'I must take that as a compliment.'

'No, no,' said Rosamond, softly whispering; and Tony laughed.

'Eustace has been ill again to-day, Tony.'

'Poor Eustace!'

'Poor Rica! I don't think I *could* love a man with the stomach-ache, Tony.'

'A nice comfortable wife you will be in affliction!'

'I mean I don't think I could love Eustace with the stomach-ache.'

'What should such a baby know about love?' Tony demanded.

'I know a great deal about it,' Rosamond affirmed.

'Tell me, then – what is your idea – how long would you expect a sane man – quite healthy-minded, nothing morbid about him – to hanker after a woman he has been told cares nothing for him and does care for someone else? How long, Rosamond?'

'Oh, I don't know,' she said tremulously. She turned her face, the sun in her brown eyes, and looked at him unmovedly smoking his pipe as though she could read the answer before she heard it from his lips. 'If he loved her really – frightfully, you know – perhaps he would always want her just as badly, Tony. Don't you think so?'

Tony took the pipe from his lips, looked at its ashes with interest, and knocked them out on the root of the tree by which he sat.

'How should I know?' he asked. 'I want to know what you think. Would it be possible, now, for a man to get over his love for one girl and begin to love another in the space of – less than a week?'

'I don't know,' said Rosamond, red as a rose, and turning away her eyes. 'Do you think that possible, Tony?'

He took out his tobacco-pouch and gave it to her to hold while he refilled his pipe. 'It's like this, dear. A man that was so easily consoled couldn't have any very strong feelings, I'm afraid. He might change his mind again, you see.'

'Oh, he wouldn't,' Rosamond cried, her eager eyes upon the face of her 'rustic youth brown with meridian toil.' 'She wouldn't – that second one would not – be such an idiot as to let him. Depend upon it, it was the first time that he mistook, Tony.'

He smiled to himself as he shook his head. 'No confidence to be placed in such a man as that,' he said. 'A nice figure he'd cut on the stage or in a novel. Hallo! *Hallo*, Rosamond! What is this?'

'This' was a procession of a dozen people approaching them across the meadow, one of whom, a woman, crowded a wheelbarrow before her.

'Someone, having pity on our generally famished condition, has killed his pig, and is bringing it for an offering.'

'It is a pig tied up in a bundle, then.'

'It is a bundle in a dark blue cotton frock and a sailor hat.'

'It is Bel!'

The girl rushed forward to meet the little advancing group. The principal figure proved to be the mother of Ivan Cattle, crowding home Bel Boyan, laid upon a little clean straw in the bottom of a dirty wheelbarrow.

'The child was too weak to walk and too heavy to carry,' the woman said, wiping the perspiration from brow and throat. 'It's a good tidy push from my house here,' she added, 'and she's a fine girl. She'd make two o' my little Everlina that's her age, but, as I say to my husban', doubtless she have been better fed.'

'But what is the matter?' Rosamond asked, wide eyes of astonishment upon the form of her sister sleeping in Mrs Cattle's wheelbarrow.

The fact that the child had gone to Mrs Cattle's cottage to see Ivan, and had suddenly become too weak to walk home, simple enough to state and easily comprehended, was set forth by Ivan's mother in a rigmarole which threatened to last the night. The shilling which should have been for the tramp, Tony put into her hand, and while she was still delivering herself of the burden of her information, Rosamond had carried the child upstairs and laid her on her bed.

'She and my Ivan have catched a chill,' Mrs Cattle ran on. ''Twas that a-shettin' of 'em up in a gig-house – which you might go for to treat the beasts of the field better – have give a shock to the symptom, follered by a chronic cold. My Ivan – he's all of a rash; you can't pick a pin for 'em; and the young lady, she come down with a shet-knife as she were wishful to give 'm. There they ha' been a-playin' all day, till I found 'em both a-settin' in one cheer asleep. A little angel, little miss, she looked, I'm sure. And when she oped her eyes at last, I found as she couldn't so much as walk.'

'Do you think we had better have a doctor?' Rosamond asked with an alarmed face.

Mrs Cattle thought no. The 'shock to the symptom' given by the gig-house explained it all, she judged. For her part, she should wait for a day or so and see how it were with Ivan. Seeing as how she had five children in the fam'ly, the parish would allow a doctor for nothing, but she questioned if her man would care for the walk of four miles to the relieving officer, and six in the opposite direction for the doctor, when his day's work was done. As for Mrs Cattle herself, she had a swellin' on her leg from gettin' about too soon after her last little un – her Georgiana – was born, which hurt her cruel when she walked on it. And after the doctor was fetched, there was to tramp the distance again for the physic. It was easy to understand one did not call in the doctor's services unless obliged.

'She's got heaps of children of her own – she should know better than I do,' Rosamond said to herself uneasily as undressed the little girl and put her to bed. 'But oh, how I do wish mother were here!'

'It is only that my head and my legs feel so funny,' Bel declared; and once in bed she seemed better.

'It's the heat of the sun. She's only very hot,' said Rica, the experienced, giving her valuable opinion. 'My poor dear Eustace, too, is nearly dead with the heat. He had only strength to drop into the arm-chair when he got in. He says he sha'n't move for the rest of the evening.'

'I've got some eggs for his tea – for all our teas!' Rosamond joyfully remembered.

She flew downstairs. Eustace, his slight figure very limp and exhausted-looking, was lying back in the Windsor chair by the fireplace. He was gazing helplessly through his glasses at Tony, who had just come in.

'I think that's my coat you're sitting on, old man,' Tony said with a certain apprehension.

'Is it only your coat? I feared there was something wrong. There was a kind of crackling noise when I sat down, and –. But I really can't get up, Tony. Whatever evil is done I will repair later on, but don't ask me to get up.'

'You've made a custard of twenty eggs, that's all,' Tony said in the calm accents of despair. 'Pray don't disturb yourself.'

Tears of anger were in Rosamond's eyes. The broken yolks of the eggs were plainly to be observed oozing from the coat pockets and dropping slowly down the legs of the chair.

'I should like to *hurt* you for it,' Rosamond said, and shook a vengeful little fist at her brother-in-law.

There was nothing for it but to sit down to the usual meal of bread and cheese and tea.

CHAPTER FIFTEEN

The Youngest Boyan Retires

IT was not until the elders were seated at the table that Bay Boyan was missed. Rosamond sought her next door, expecting to find her on the dirty floor playing with the beloved Joshua. Not a trace of her.

'She have trailed off somewheers with my little un,' the ill-tempered neighbour said. 'All this week I ha' been in a faver, not knowin' wheer my child was decoyed to.'

'Didn't Joshua come home from school with the rest?' Rosamond asked, and was told that not only had he not come home, but that he had not been to afternoon school at all.

'Him and that theer little un o' yours trailed off after mornin' school,' Mrs Nobbs said.

Here Dan offered information. They had gone off in the dinner-hour. He had seen them a goin' hand-in-hand down the road.

Rosamond and Rica looked at each other with dismayed, remorseful faces when the younger girl carried this intelligence next door. Not since eight in the morning had either seen or thought of the loved little sister for whose well-being they were responsible. Not since twelve, it appeared, fuller inquiry being made, had she been seen of mortal eye!

The sisters, once alarmed, were nearly frantic with terror. Bel, ill in bed, was left in sole charge of the cottage while they and Eustace and his brother searched the village. Mrs Nobbs, called on to join the quest, refused.

'Wheeriver your little un's trailed to, there's my Josher – po'r little onconscious lamb!' she said. She had her husband's supper to see to; her maternal fears were not easily aroused.

One going in one direction and one in another, Bay's relations had soon explored the village. They had been to the school, had been to the homes of the school children, had called in at the shop, and looked through the windows of the church. All without result. Never since the two had set forth hand-in-hand from the school gate had sign of the little pair been seen.

'They have strayed into the fields and fallen asleep there,' Eustace said, speaking with confidence before his wife and sister-in-law, but eyeing his brother with doubtful looks. He had heard of children being lost in a field of corn, he said.

'Let all the men turn out,' Rica said. She was white, but not helpless in this emergency. It seemed to be Rosamond who was silent, shaken, almost benumbed with fear. 'Let them scour every field. Tell them we will pay them, Eustace. Nothing will be too much for us to pay if they find the children.'

So in a little time the quiet place resounded in that silent hour with the noise of trampling feet, of calling voices, and the loud clanging of a bell which one of the men pulled of a cherry tree in the orchard, where it had been hung to scare the birds. But no little voices called in answer. The clanging of the rusty bell sounded, cracked and empty, across the vacant fields.

'They've strayed further than they knew to pluck a posy, and we shall find 'em fell asleep under some hedgerow,' the men said hopefully to each other.

But although they tramped watchful-eyed by many a nook, soft with moss and fragrant with thyme, offering a pleasant resting-place for childhood's slumber, past many a bank gay with poppies, white campion, pale nautia, the red, white and blue of the summer fields, no trace was found of the lost children.

And always in Tony's face, as Rosamond searched it for comforting reassurance, spite of its carefully-carried front of confidence, there was, to her who read it with such intimate eyes, a background of a possible horror. The terror that he tried to banish from his heart lurked in his eyes.

At the gate of a wheat field, through which a dozen men had walked at regular distances each from each, with small heed of the crop ready for harvest, Tony drew his brother apart.

'Don't speak of it to the girls,' he said. 'I met a brutal-looking, poor wretch – a tramp – on the road where the children were last seen. He looked hungry enough to be desperate. I'm going to follow up the tramp.'

He had to pass the Rectory gate on his way, and standing by it, his hat on the back of his head, his hands in his trousers pockets, was the youth upon whom he had called the evening before.

'Hi!' said Hetherington, familiarly accosting the tall young man in the soiled white flannels who was hurrying past. 'Are they playing some game, I say, ringing the bell and shouting?'

Tony stopped. It was possible this foolish-looking youth, who worked his mouth in such curious fashion about his narrow face, might have information to give. 'They are trying to find two children who are lost. They passed by here some time in the morning; a tiny pair, going hand-in-hand. You don't know anything about them?'

Hetherington blinked frantically, and shook his head. 'You're the person that hit me on the cheek last night,' he said. 'I say, I'll go along with you, if you like, and look for the kiddies.'

Without either accepting or refusing his escort, Tony went hurriedly on, and the clergyman's son kept alongside.

'Ma and pa have gone to the town to buy me *Comic Cuts*,' he said as he walked along, making tremendous exertions with his unruly legs to keep up to Tony. 'I like *Comic Cuts*, don't you? Pictures, you know. I *laugh!* Ma and pa told me not to stir away till they came back, but I like to walk along with you, if you don't mind.'

Tony expressed himself pleased with his company. 'I can't talk because my mind is full,' he said. 'But you can talk if you like. And keep your eyes open, will you?'

Hetherington gave the curious sort of strangled crow which did duty for him for a laugh. 'My eyes are pretty well open,' he announced. 'I'm not clever at books, you know. Are you? I had to leave school because I was in the form with the smallest boys, and they laughed so. I liked them – I didn't mind. But they laughed, so the master told pa I'd better leave. I haven't got that sort of learning. No. Have you, I say? But I can see things, and hear 'em too. I hear when the servants' sweethearts come at night to the kitchen window. I don't let on to ma, you know. Would you, I say, would you?'

Tony thought that was a matter to be left to Hetherington's own judgment.

'Well, I don't. But sometimes – when I want a lark, you know – I saunter out and catch 'em. The servants don't mind. They know I don't tell tales. They give me a kiss sometimes. I say, what are you looking through the hedge for? There's a ditch the other side. You don't think the kiddies have fallen in the ditch, do you?'

Tony turned from the gapped thorn-hedge to his companion. 'Look here, you seem to be a bright chap,' he said. 'Did you happen to see a tramp pass your gate to-day – a dirty, outcast, miserable-looking, poor wretch?'

'You think he's cut their throats and flung them in the ditch?' cried Hetherington, brightly, in the alert tone of making an interesting discovery. 'I say, let me take the ditches. You keep along the road and I take the ditches over the fences. If they're there I'd like to be the one to find 'em!'

In this way they travelled for a couple of miles, Tony asking questions of the few people he met, Hetherington talking to himself with knowing looks, and now and then a crow of mirth to testify to the exuberance of his feelings. Once he found a bunch of field-flowers, gathered and flung down, whose stalks looked as if they had been grasped in a hot hand. He passed them over the hedge for inspection, and Tony, looking at them with pitiful eyes, pulled them through the silk handkerchief which knotted his trousers at the waist.

Always there tramped the road beside him the figure of the vagrant with his brutalised, hungry face, his haggard, furtive eyes. 'I felt ashamed that the poor devil filled me with such loathing,' he said to himself, and he shuddered at that persistent visionary companionship. In spite of himself there arose continually in his mind the ghastly tales of the murder of little children in lonely country places for the sake of the clothes upon their backs and the few ha'pence in their pockets. The idea of the tramp had taken hold of his mind and possessed it, and the man's heart was sick with fear. A mile farther and there came to him a yell from the field on his left hand. Looking over the hedge he saw his companion in the quest, not just on the other side of the fence as he had expected, but half-way across a field, shouting to him, and wildly waving his hand.

Every vestige of colour forsook Tony Patten's healthy face. 'God! he has found them,' he said.

He vaulted the low hedge, and ran to the spot, feeling weak as a girl at the prospect of what was before him.

'What is it?' he asked, but asked with a joyful relief; for the field, which had been hay, and was shorn of the crop, was bare before him, and empty of the little murdered forms he had expected to see.

Hetherington held a white bag in his hand. 'Here's this,' he said. 'P'r'aps they had their money in it and the tramp didn't want the bag.'

Tony snatched the thing from his hand. 'They had bread and butter in it,' he said. He had seen Rosamond filling it for Bay in the morning. 'They must have gone this way.'

Hetherington gloated upon the bag. 'I don't see any blood on it,' he said. 'I expect he's dragged 'em farther on. What's that big place over there?' he asked, and pointed to a large building across a few more fields, just visible in embowering trees.

Tony looked, and looked again. 'It looks like the back of Bunwick Hall,' he said. 'There must be a short cut to it across these fields. Everyone's away – the place is empty – the child would not know the way –'

'Let's go and look,' said Hetherington, his mouth actively at work. 'P'r'aps he did it in an outhouse, you know, and carried the bodies through a window. Better than hiding 'em in a ditch, eh? I say,' making heroic efforts to keep up to Tony, who was now running across the field. 'When we've found 'em we'll go after the police together. Pa and ma wouldn't let me if they knew it – but I like to be with you, you're so strong, and it's such a lark!'

⁂

For another hour after Tony had left them the search continued. In the west the orange sky of evening died away, the gushes of song from the throats of birds hid in the hedgerow and the foliage of trees grew hushed, the sober hues of evening and its silence were upon them, and all watched the approach of oncoming night with terror.

Rosamond, the colour blanched from her round, brown cheeks, her bright eyes strained and wild-looking, ran back to the Cherry-tree Cottages. It was just possible that Bel might help with a suggestion; she would know better than the older ones what was likely to have attracted the little feet.

The girl ran across the fields. Her light, springy step was gone, she stumbled at every little inequality in the soil, her feet were like lead. It seemed impossible to her to accomplish the weary distance from field to field. The dews of late evening were beginning to moisten the earth; far in the opal sky a star or two faintly showed. Rosamond hated them – hated the friendly fields, the familiar slope and valley, tree and hedgerow; all nature was her enemy, smiling at her misery and silently withholding that which she longed to know.

Her lips moved as she ran, and her mother's name and Bay's were always on them. 'Oh, mother! Poor mother! My mother! Little Bay! Our darling, little Bay! Mother, forgive me! Forgive!'

As she neared the cottages, a sound of confused voices fell on her ear, and she discovered that in the garden of the Nobbs's cottage a sympathising crowd had gathered. Mrs Nobbs, aroused from her apathy at last by well-meant attempts at consolation, sat on a chair within the open door, her dirty apron wrung into a twisted rope in her two hands, and screamed aloud.

Rosamond's fears leapt to the worst. The children had been found, and were dead.

The crowd of women choking up the little garden space made way for her. She could not speak, but looked fearfully around.

"'Tis hard on the poor mother,' a stout woman, who was snuffling and weeping, said. 'No one can't a-wonder at her a-takin' on, him bein' the lessest of 'em all.'

'He ain't even in the bur'al club,' another said. 'Come to ha' been Dan, now, or Sairey, both on 'em's in, and 'twould ha' been a consolation.'

'Is he found?' Rosamond asked with her white lips. 'Is he dead?'

'Take her away!' screamed Mrs Nobbs. 'Don't let my eyes light on her. If so be as she'd look'd arter her little un as she oughter ha' looked, she wouldn't ha' trailed off wi' my Josher.'

Rosamond grasped with both hands the arm of a woman standing by to keep herself from falling. 'Have they found him? Do they know where he is?' she gasped.

It was Mrs Chaney to whom Rosamond was clinging. 'My dear,' she said, 'don't you go for to take to heart what po'r Mrs Nobbs say in her mis'ry. 'Tis a grief, indeed, miss, to lose a child, and, if so be 'tis as she say, a dreadful death for the po'r blessed lamb to die; though, the Lord bein' merciful, he's out of his pain by now.'

'How? Tell me!'

'Down the well. They ha' both on 'em toppled down the well,' a hoarse woman, with a more direct mode of expression, explained.

Mrs Chaney put her arms about the girl who was holding her. ''Twas the mother's thought, my dear,' she told her in the smooth and placid accents which so infuriated her neighbour. 'Soon as she grasped he were gone, "The well," she say. 'Tis for all the world like old Becky Hunt; when she heared as her sailor-son were lost at sea, "Sure enough he be drownded," she say, and sure enough he were.'

Rosamond broke away from the restraining arm, and threw herself forward upon Mrs Nobbs in her chair, still twisting and wringing her lilac apron into a rope.

'Why the well?'

Mrs Nobbs looked up at the girl, who had her by the shoulder and was shaking her to attention, and suddenly stopped screaming to explain. 'Dan, he see 'em there once afore,' she said. 'Your little un was a-tryin' to h'ist up my Josher to look in at the farns a-growin' up the sides. There

105

ain't no mander o' doubt but what they've both on 'em toppled in th' well.'

So far coherently and in the voice of calmness; then again loud screams, and Josher's name shrieked forth upon the evening air.

'The well,' Rosamond repeated, but no sound came, only the words formed themselves upon her lips. She never doubted. She seemed to see the children hanging over the edge, and the heavy-headed Josher overbalancing himself, Bay's desperate efforts to save him ending in her own destruction. She pushed the women aside, flinging out her arms, careless of what they encountered, to clear her path. They followed her as she ran through the little garden and across the field to that spot where the old cottages had been pulled down, and the well, uncovered, and with crumbling wall, was placed amid a high growth of nettles and rank grass.

'Sure's God, she be a-goin' to fling herself arter 'em,' the stout woman said. 'Bring a pail, b'or,' to her more swift-footed neighbour, who at once retraced her steps to obey her. 'Bring a pail!'

'They was all won'erful set on that there little un,' Mrs Chaney said; 'and though she's but young, doubtless she have her feelins.'

''Tain't to say she ha' got a mother's feelin's,' another woman objected, as Mrs Nobbs's loud scream followed them from where she still sat twisting her apron in the cottage door. 'We know what a mother's feelin's is, and 'tain't in nature she ha' got 'em.'

'Ah, sorrer's a diff'rent how-d'ye-do when there's money to fill the gaps,' the hoarse woman attested, and spat as she ran.

'Is it a deep well?' Rosamond asked, flinging her white young face round on them. 'Is it certain they would be killed?'

It was Mrs Chaney who was nearest to her, and who answered. 'If 'tweren't the water, 'twould be the suffercatin' mis'ry o' the place, my dear,' she explained. 'There's the chanst if they weren't drownded they'd be only onsensible, but, anyways, they'd be past all arthly help, po'r lambs, by now; and don't you go for to have no other thought, Miss Rosamon'?'

'I'm going down to see,' Rosamond said.

There was an outcry at this. 'The chain ain't strong enough to bear the weight of a child, let alone a fine grown young woman sech as you be.'

'The chain's broke and mended wi' rope. 'Twould be a-throwin' away your life, gal,' the hoarse-voiced woman cried loudly.

'I'm going,' said Rosamond.

They were clustered round the well. Going on her knees, one of the women looked down the dark sides, where the green hart's tongue growing among the bricks glistened cool and moist, to the black, still water below.

'Josher! Josher!' she called, and the woman nervously as the sepulchrally-echoed name was flung back in their faces.

Rosamond stood at the handle and resolutely unwound the chain for a yard or so, and attached the bucket. 'Hold it fast for me,' she said.

But they held her instead, and one of them, looking back at the cottages, waved an excited arm and shouted aloud for help. 'There's two men a-runnin',' she gasped, and frantically waved her apron and cried, 'Hi! Hi! Help!'

Rosamond fought with the women and pushed them aside. She pulled the bucket on a level with the mouldering parapet. She leant over and clutched the chain. 'Let go!' she cried, and struck at the hands which held her – only the feeble, irresolute hands of people unused to defy authority.

'God A'mighty! ketch hold o' the handle, some on yer,' the hoarse-voiced woman cried, and two of the women clung to it.

Two men, in response to cries for help, were running across the meadow. Rosamond, with eyes which consciously saw nothing but the well and Bay's little loved body drowned in its black and ugly depth, saw them – a tall, white-clad figure which, under other circumstances, she would have recognised at a glance among countless thousands, and a small, narrow youth, considerably in the background, whose large hat hung at the back of his head, and whose thin ankles showed between his shoes and the bottoms of his trousers as he ran.

Even in the girl's half-crazed, wholly desperate state, to get into the bucket was no easy matter. From the broken side of the parapet she made the attempt, but, as soon as one foot was in the pail swung away from her.

'Hold it!' she said, in the fierce tone they were somehow afraid to disobey. A couple of women knelt down and held the bucket close to the wall.

Both feet were in now, and she clinging to the chain above. 'Let go!' she cried. But someone, hoarse and authoritative, and near at hand now, cried 'Hold on!' And the two women clinging to the handle, and the two who held the bucket, obeyed the latter voice.

Rosamond swayed her body in the pail, trying to free herself. 'Let go!' she cried again; and as she felt an arm seize her from behind and pass tightly round her waist, she struggled with a strength which bade fair to hurl her to destruction.

—⟡—

Tony's voice had failed him in his run across the meadow. It was with an effort he brought out the panting whisper, 'The children are all right – Bay is all right.'

The mad struggle to escape from him ceased instantly. He was holding her with her back to him; she could not see his face. 'Swear it,' she said.

'I swear,' said Tony, and she began to tremble violently within his arm. A great terror of her own danger seized her and bewildered her senses.

'Oh, save me! save me!' she cried, in a panic of unreasoning fear.

It seemed an age to the young man that he held her convulsively clasped to him without an effort to lift her from her position. In many a shuddering day-dream and many a nightmare, he lived through that minute again in which it seemed that his strength had shamefully deserted him in his uttermost need, in which his bones seemed turned to water in his limbs, and his sinews were unstrung, and he told himself that he never could recapture the power necessary to lift the girl from her place of danger and set her safe on the firm earth again.

No sooner did they see this feat accomplished – and to their observation there had appeared no delay – than the women set off, running with stiff limbs but glad hearts, across the meadow to bear the good news to Mrs Nobbs. Hetherington looked after them a minute, as if debating whether to follow them, but relinquished the idea of doing so in favour of remaining by the well to watch the young man and the girl.

Rosamond stood up for a moment, still within the support of Tony's arms, then slipped from them to the ground, where, putting her hands before her face, she began violently to cry.

Hetherington watched her, his mouth screwed into a button, or expanding in one straight line from ear to ear, and nodded his head over her. He was enjoying himself finely altogether that evening; he had seldom been more interested.

Tony's eyes rested for a minute on the girl at his feet, and then moved to the youth before him. 'I am very much obliged to you for your companionship – and what you've done,' he said. 'I won't detain you any longer now. I'm sure you're anxious to be getting home.'

Hetherington demurred. 'Pa and ma won't know where I've been. I shall say in the garden; it'll be all right.'

Rosamond dropped her shielding hand for a second and looked at the narrow youth. 'Send him away! send him away!' she cried hysterically. 'Why don't you go away?' she asked, addressing young Mr Dodman himself in a burst of tearful anger; then she covered her face again and continued to sob.

Hetherington winked at Tony and nodded his head in a particularly knowing fashion. 'I know,' he said, 'I can see what she wants. I'm going.'

He sauntered off very slowly, and with evident reluctance, turning at every few paces to look back at Tony, who had forgotten him. He had sat down with his back to the well by Rosamond's side, and put his arm about her shoulder and made her lean upon him.

'How came you to be such a fool, Rosamond?' he asked.

She cried on. It seemed that she could never stop crying.

'Are you so unhappy because your little sister is found?' he asked her at length.

'It is because I nearly died,' she sobbed. 'If you had not come at that instant I should be dead now – dead at the bottom of that horrid, horrid well! And I should hate to leave you all, Tony. Oh, how I should hate to leave you all!'

'You should have thought of that before,' Tony said sensibly. 'Didn't you think of it? Didn't you say to yourself, "If I trust myself to this mouldy rope and rust-eaten chain, I shall never see daylight and Tony Patten again?"'

'I nev-er thought of the – daylight.'

'Nor of me?'

'Not – for a second.'

'Rosamond!'

'I thought of mother, and of darling, darling little Bay at the bottom of the well.'

'Well, the next time you're going to be so silly, think of me, will you?'

'Where are they? Where did you find them?' she asked him.

And while she continued to shake like a leaf, and sat with her face hidden in her hands, lest he should see it convulsed by emotion, he gave her a brief history of the search which had ended so happily. He told her how he and the young Dodman were led to visit the deserted house of the Boyans; how they speedily found that neither of the servants left in charge had seen or heard anything of the children; and how he was coming away in despair, but that Hetherington insisted on going over the house. Truth to say, the youth had a wild hope that he would find the children murdered and flung under the bed.

It was in a bedroom they came upon them, but in, not under, the bed. In her own little crib the youngest Boyan was lying, fully dressed, but sound asleep. On the coverlet, across her feet, the dolly Maude was placed, and closely clasped in her arms, his little, spotty, unwholesome face on the same pillow with that flower-like little face of her own, was the form of the big-headed Josher.

Tony had deemed it wise to leave the children undisturbed in the care of the old housekeeper, who was one of Bay's chief worshippers, while he had a horse put in the dog-cart, and himself and young Mr Dodman, suffering from a little depression for the moment due to a natural disappointment in the *dénouement*, were driven at once to Dulditch.

'Where, if you'd arrived five minutes later, you'd have found me dead,' said Rosamond, still shivering and tearful.

'A dem'd demp corpse,' commented Tony, who was averse from sentiment.

It was thus that the youngest and wisest of the Boyans threw up the tedious and, at times, painful game the family had taken upon itself to play.

CHAPTER SIXTEEN

For the Last Time

IN the course of another twenty-four hours, and by dint of walking for half the night, Ivan Cattle's father secured the benefit of medical attendance for his son.

The doctor, by good luck, took Dulditch on an early round, and made Ivan one of his first cases. Having pronounced the boy to be suffering from measles, and given directions for the father to walk the twelve miles there and back to his surgery for the necessary medicine, he inquired if there were any more cases he would be likely to be called in to attend. Hearing of the probable one at Cherry-tree Cottages, he drove there and found Bel.

The men were once more at their turnip-hoeing beneath the relentless sun. The girls were terrified to find their sister suffering from measles. The doctor was their own medical man, and an old friend of the

110

family besides. It was in accordance with his advice that they decided at once to telegraph for their mother.

'The child can't be properly nursed here,' he said. 'We must take the risk of getting her to her home, and her mother must come and see to her removal.'

He did not hesitate to tell them what he thought of the Experiment when it was explained to him.

'It's only through the *habit* of semi-starvation that the system accommodates itself to the condition,' he said. 'Rosamond here is probably strong enough to have escaped evil effects –'

'Nought comes to no harm,' Rosamond reminded him easily.

'But Rica is weak through improper and insufficient food. She also will probably be down with measles before many days are over. Serve her right – serve you all right! What's that husband of yours thinking of, Mrs Patten?'

'Eustace,' said Rica, tragically, 'is, I am sure, ill, doctor. He ate no breakfast this morning, and I saw him stagger as he walked across the field to his work.'

The doctor nodded. 'About two days more of want of food and of unaccustomed work under such a sun will about finish him. Serve him right!' said the man of medicine, unfeelingly. 'What right had he, with his physique, and a wife with no more staying power than a chicken, to engage in such a prank?'

'Eustace thinks,' said Rica, looking with a little offence upon the practical man, 'that we have no business to ask a section of society, our inferiors only by the accident of birth, to exist under circumstances beneath which we could not exist. He wished to prove that what seemed impossible, and yet was done around us every day, was not only possible but – but agreeable.'

'Well?'

'It certainly isn't agreeable,' Rosamond avowed.

'It's the age of meddling,' the doctor said, 'and your husband, fine fellow as he is, is infected by the meddling spirit, Rica. Tell him, with my compliments, to look after you and himself, and *to leave things alone,* my dear. That's my prescription for him and his generation – leave things alone –'

'You and daddy think alike on these matters, I know,' said Rica, 'but Eustace says he is afraid to abide by the easy thing. Eustace wants to know –'

'Eustace is a nuisance,' Rosamond declared. 'Doctor, stop and see me scrub the bricks.' She had rolled up her sleeves over her smooth, brown arms, her pail was already beside her on the floor. 'Look here!' she said, and stepped back and took a running step or two and sprang over it. 'I'm so happy I'm going home to-night that I could jump over the moon,' she declared.

'Get a little stimulant for your husband if he can't eat,' the doctor said in parting to Rica. He was frankly of the old-fashioned school, and believed in the invigorating effect of a little good port or even of a bottle of stout; he was much loved by the poor, therefore, for whom he ordered those luxuries with a liberality which did not always meet with the approbation of the Board of Guardians. He undertook himself to telegraph for Mrs Boyan and to meet her at the station in his close carriage, in which the child could be moved.

—◦◇◦—

The part of the doctor's remarks which related to the stimulant was repeated by Rica to Mrs Chaney, who, good and well-meaning soul that she was, appeared shortly afterwards with a bottle under her arm. She was breathless and panting from her errand.

'I ha' been down town' (down town was that part of the village where Mrs Barrett's shop was situated) 'and begged a bottle o' my Aunt Rhody's rhubarb wind,' she explained, and she laid a hand on that part of her anatomy where she wrongfully supposed her throbbing heart to be. 'She make it herself, so you may know for sure there's nothing harmful in it, and 'tis won'erful sustainin', as Mist' Patten will find it, if I may make so bold as to offer it to him. My husban' when he've a cold in 's back, where it mostly strike the man, say as how, Aunt Rhody's rhubarb wind, that send a glow right t'rough him!'

On the day previous the weekly pig had died in Dulditch, and Rosamond, in defiance of Eustace's prohibition, strengthened in her determination by her own exceeding hunger, and by the fact that her mother was coming and her emancipation near at hand, had carried off in triumph a joint from Mrs Barrett.

'If you don't give it me peaceably, I shall fight you for it,' she said. 'I stole a tin of salmon the other night because you would not be reasonable. You would not like me to turn murderer as well as thief, would you, Mrs Barrett?'

'I never see sech a young lady!' Mrs Barrett declared with awe. 'Between your goin's-on, and between what Mr Patten's written orders to me is, I'm at my wits' ends.'

So Rosamond helped her out of her dilemma by seizing upon a joint which lay conveniently near her on the counter, and by making off with it.

''Tis best so,' said Mrs Barrett, philosophically, to her next customer, relating, with much repetition of circumstance and enlargement of detail, the story. 'They ha' got it to ate, so their ma'll be pleased, and I di'n't, so to say, give my consent, so Mr Patten can't find no fault.'

'Surely, surely Eustace will enjoy the pork,' Rica said.

She was so attracted by the smell of the roasting meat, and so anxious that it should be nicely cooked for Eustace, that although she had to sit by Bel's bedside, her heart, as she pathetically explained to Rosamond, was 'in the oven.'

Poor Bel lay with hot and aching head in the little bedroom with its hideous, drab-papered walls, upon which she hated to turn her feverish eyes, but from which she could not keep them. She was too ill even to be glad overmuch that 'mother' was coming and she going home.

'We will never play at this ugly game again, Rica,' she said more than once. 'Oh, it has been so very ugly.'

Always afterwards, when the Patten Experiment was referred to in Bel's hearing, she saw at once those ghastly low walls of drab, blotched here and there at regular intervals with meaningless dabs of a frightful, vulgar blue; she saw how the sunlight, which would come in at that corner the towel pinned across the window failed to cover, fired painfully the tiny square of looking-glass hung above the photograph of horrid Nurse Brunton's uniformed son; so that when Bel closed her aching eyes she saw them – picture and mirror – flaming with just as agonising vividness through her throbbing lids. She felt her throat again parched with thirst for which there was no relief at hand; she smelt the nauseating smell of the roasting meat pervading the little cramped space; and Rica's careful movements over the bare boards once more jarred the sick and aching head.

And, after all, Eustace could not eat the pork. He affected to be very joyful when its odours, and the odour of the cabbage enhancing its toothsomeness, met his nostrils. He sat down, looking very leaden about the lips; and, with Rica's anxious eyes fixed on him, he accepted a liberal supply, but he only played with it, Rica saw very well. He cut up the food and placed some on his fork, but, having got the portion half way to his mouth, laid it down again, and slipping his hands into his trousers pockets, sat huddled together in the attitude of a man too exhausted to sit upright.

'It looks a little rich, darling,' he said to his wife, sickly regarding the food he could not eat. 'Be very careful how you partake of it, Rica. I think, for my part, a crust of bread will suit me better.'

But when this was given him, he only crumbled the bread with stiff but shaking fingers, and did not eat.

Then Rica bethought her of Aunt Rhoda's wine. They had no wine-glasses, so she poured him out a tumblerful. 'It is home-made, so it can't hurt you,' she said.

Finding that it was of cottage brew, and moreover was given by one poor person to another, he had no scruples, but drank it off, being very thirsty.

'I think I'll take my portion of bread to the open air,' he said. 'The fumes of the pork, delicious as it smells, are just a little upsetting.'

Rosamond, anxious to make a festival of the occasion, would have poured wine into the other glasses, but Rica pounced upon the bottle. It was given to Eustace. He might want further stimulating, as Dr Oldman had said. The wine should be kept for Eustace.

So she carried out another tumblerful to the poor gentleman lying under the shade of the big ash tree at Mrs Nobbs's corner; and Eustace thanked her and eagerly quaffed the beverage.

When the time came for the men to go to their afternoon labours, Rica reported that her husband was asleep.

'Let him sleep,' Tony advised. 'He's got about enough of this, I think. The longer we keep him asleep the better.'

Tony had decided, for his own part, that he had also had enough. 'I reckon I have given out of me the value of your father's eleven shillings in one way or another,' he said. 'If I haven't been hoeing his turnips for a whole week – in fact, I feel in the weariness of my mind, the aching of my bones, the raw state of my skin, I have been at it for a century. By yesterday's proceedings ten years at least were taken off my life; and my peaceful, unbroken slumber is destroyed, I suppose, for ever.'

'All night long,' he said to Rosamond, 'I was lifting you out of that accursed tub, and at the critical moment you were always swaying away from me, or slipping out of my hold. Or you became heavy beyond the power of human arm to lift, or my strength left me, flowing away from me like water. I woke up ten times in cold sweats; and once I thought I was yelling your name and must have wakened the house. Did you hear me doing it?'

Rosamond had not heard him. No one, she was quite sure, had heard him, an assurance which gave Tony great satisfaction.

114

'To hear a man bawling out a girl's name in the middle of the night might create a false impression,' Tony said.

No. He would not help Rosamond to wash up the plates, he would not 'rid up' the floor, or even scour the saucepans! The fact was he had had enough of the absurd farce. It hadn't been funny in the least, and a week of his holiday had been spoilt. If there had been profit or enjoyment in it, the whole thing was not yet sufficiently in perspective for him to see it.

And now, he who had his living to get, and nothing but his good name to depend on, must look forward to seeing that name appear in the newspapers as the name of a poacher, and must familiarise himself with the probability of spending the rest of his holiday in prison!

The next time Eustace wanted to make an ass of himself, and Eustace's wife's people supported him in that ambition, they could set their minds at rest! He, Tony Patten, would not be found in the neighbourhood.

Then he went out and smoked his pipe at the gate and watched the proceedings of Josher, whom his mother would not trust to go to school that day, lest he should again 'trail off' in the companionship of the dangerous Bay – for her part, safe at home at Bunwick Hall, with the dear doll Maude for companion, and firmly resolved in her mind never to go near Chelly-t'ee Cottage again. Josher, looked after by his mother, was much in a like position to Josher taking care of himself. However, to give him his due, he was not an adventurous child, nor an unruly, and, no one being by to take him by the hand and lead him into mischief, was likely to remain inactive on that spot of earth on which he first fell down for ever.

In order to ensure his interest and diversion, he had been presented by his thoughtful mother with the key of the front door. This for some time he placidly sucked, breathing hard, and gazing out over the wide plain of grass which surrounded him with vacant, pale eyes. For change of occupation he presently converted the key into a spade, and dug up roots of grass and lumps of soil, now and again diverting his tool to its former use and enjoying a mingled flavour of mould and iron very agreeable to the palate.

With these occupations he was stolidly content, until a small black beetle, making a journey across the scorched grass, took the boy's bare leg in its way. Josher watched the course of the insect across his defenceless limb in soundless terror, until it safely reached brown grass again. Then with a yell of anguish the child arose and fled from the vicinity of the beetle.

115

He ran with tearless howlings and widespread arms to the corner of the Cherry-tree Cottages where the big ash-tree was, where Eustace had stretched himself in the shade, and he hurled himself against that gentleman's prone body and fell over it.

This did not arouse Eustace, but it completely flabbergasted Josher, whose screams stopped instantly, all his powers focused in the one condition of feeling astonishment. He picked himself up slowly, and sat himself down as close as he could accommodate his person to the unconscious man's head. Then, having gazed, open-mouthed and stertorous, upon the features of the gentleman whom he had never enjoyed the advantage of seeing at such close quarters before, he proceeded to investigate further by the sense of touch, poking his dirty, small fingers into eyes and mouth.

Tony, who had swung open the little gate upon which he leaned in order the better to enjoy the proceedings, observed him now in the act of inserting the door-key between the Reverend Eustace's parted lips, and was about to interfere. But at that critical moment Rica, who had been watching over her husband's welfare from behind the impromptu blind in Bel's room, came down with a rush, flew out like a whirlwind, and, seizing upon the unsuspecting Josher like a nightmare, flung him afar off with the strength of a Samson.

It was with such a mixture of similes that Tony afterwards described the descent of his sister-in-law. He was laughing at the sight and softly calling to Rosamond to come and enjoy the fun, when Rica, on her knees beside her husband, called to him in the quick accents of alarm. She looked up at him when he reached her with her sweet, frightened eyes.

'He won't wake,' she said. 'I've tried – I can't wake him. Oh! He isn't dead, Tony? He isn't dead!'

'He surely would not snore so loud if he were dead,' Tony said. But he looked down upon the man whose heavy, inert hand Rica was caressing with an awakened curiosity. And having looked, he stooped and lifted his brother further into the shade, and taking off his own jacket, laid it over his shoulders.

'He'll be all right when he wakes, poor old chap,' he said. 'Let him be, Rica.'

'Ah! Ten to one he've got a touch of the sun, po'r gentleman,' Mrs Chaney, prompt as ever to reach the spot, declared. 'He's unsensed like, time being.'

'Looks like it,' Tony said gravely. 'The symptoms are not alarming, but in these cases there's nothing like letting the patient sleep it off.'

He persuaded Rica to go up to her patient again, leaving her husband quite undisturbed; and he himself, having smoked his pipe out, turned his back on the heavily-sleeping man and made his way back into the kitchen.

It was clean and neat again, the fire of sticks (the hundredweight of coal was finished long ago) beginning to crackle; the kettle, fresh filled, had been placed on the stove; and Rosamond, the dark blue cotton sleeves turned up to her shoulders, stooped over a basin of cold well water placed on the little round table in the window, bathing face and arms and hands.

She was always indulging in temporary grievances against Tony. She had one on now, and did not speak to him, but continued to splash the water over her pretty bare arms, and bending down her head to the basin to drown her red-brown face in the clear, sparkling water which Tony himself had drawn not so very long ago from the depths of the earth.

And the sun, flickering in through the geranium screen in the window, lighted in dazzling patches upon her so easily-illumined hair, and danced in sunny glimmerings on the dark blue of her cotton dress, and seemed to linger lovingly on the girlish arms glistening wet, while Tony sat upon the corner of the table and swung one shortened leg and looked on.

'Well, I suppose this is the finish, Rosamond,' he said.

'Thank Heaven!' said Rosamond, with pious alacrity.

'I don't know. I've a notion that, back teaching those infernal boys, I shall begin to think our week in this little place uncommonly jolly.'

'You've altered your tone considerably.'

'When a man's smoked himself into a good skin you shouldn't cast up old grudges against him, Rosamond. You've been a brick of a girl. I suppose, if I'd lived with you for a year at Bunwick Hall I should never have known what stuff you're made of as I know now.'

'And now you do know, what then?' Rosamond asked in her embarrassing way of putting what might be considered leading questions.

She had her face in the towel, scrubbing her fresh cheeks into rosy brightness; she paused in the occupation and peeped at him with shining, brown eyes over the towel as she asked the question.

He swung his leg, looked out of doors, and made no answer.

'You would have been always dangling attendance on Mary, who never wanted you – that's why you would have known nothing of me,' Rosamond informed him with lofty scorn, and proceeded vigorously to rub her cheeks again.

117

'At anyrate, I should not have enjoyed the privilege of seeing you perform your toilette before me in this entirely artless and unapologetic fashion.'

She flung the towel across the kitchen and began tearing at her sleeves to unroll them, and perhaps he wished he had spared her the taunt.

'Can I go up to my room when Bel is asleep there?' she demanded, with flaming cheeks. 'How does it hurt you, I should like to know, to see me wash my face?'

'I haven't complained. I think it an awfully pretty sight.'

'You are a fool,' said Rosamond, with much irritation and small dignity.

'Come here, Baby, and let me unwind your hair.'

'I don't want your help any longer,' Rosamond declared, and began with impetuous fingers to pull the hairpins from her braids. 'I have been worked to death to-day, and you didn't care. You smoked and smoked, and wouldn't even so much as wash a saucepan!'

'And I don't deserve any reward? Nevertheless, let me do it, Rosamond. 'Tis for the last time.'

So she, who always quickly relented, placed herself with her back to him as he half sat on the table, and slowly, with a touch that lingered because (perhaps) the work of both was done and there was no reason to be in a hurry any more, he loosened and unwound the heavy hair.

'You have played at being a woman for a little time,' he said very gently. 'The game is too hard and too dangerous for you as yet. You must go back and be a child again, will you, Rosamond?'

She was silent, weakened for the moment by the alteration in his voice.

'Will you, dear? For another year, at least? Till I come again?'

And Rosamond, stumbling over the words, in a hurried, eager whisper, promised that she would – that she would do anything he liked if only he would come again.

It was while such engrossing conversation was going on at the back of the house that a carriage, driven noiselessly over the meadow grass, stopped before the front door of the centre one of the Cherry-tree Cottages. Rica, seeing it from her post of observation at poor Bel's window, flew downstairs, and, before greeting father or mother, caught the doctor by the hand.

'Come to Eustace,' she cried. 'He is lying there – unconscious – like a log. Tony is so cruel, he won't let me keep with him. I don't know if it is dangerous – he has a touch of the sun, doctor.'

But it was Rica's father who, seeing the prostrate body as the carriage stopped, reached it first; he bent over the unconscious Eustace and the unconscious Eustace snored in his face. Mr Boyan raised himself and touched his son-in-law with a contemptuous foot.

'The man's drunk,' he said.

He glared in Rica's face as if she (as indeed was the case, had he but known) had been responsible for that ignominy. Then, turning a fiercely scornful back on expostulation and protestation, he strode up the gay garden, brushing the phloxes, the delphiniums, the sunflowers with an angry shoulder, and into the house where his little Bel lay ill. His little Bel! His favourite! She was his favourite while ill; each of his daughters in that condition was his favourite.

He made his way through the front room – Nurse Brunton's pride – unheeding its splendours of shining chair, of gay carpet, unspoilt by human occupancy; he pushed open with impatient hand the door leading to the kitchen.

And there, in the blaze of sunlight entering by the open door, through which the small gravelled yard, the drab-painted pump, the strip of garden-ground ending in the fence of scarlet-runners were visible, he found Tony Patten seated upon the corner of the table engaged in leisurely arranging the tresses of his daughter Rosamond's hair.

CHAPTER SEVENTEEN

I'll Bid you Good-bye

ALTHOUGH she was back in the home she had never gladly left, and had all her children around her once more, poor Mrs Boyan had rather a bad time of it that evening.

'It's been all your doing, and I hope you're proud of your work!' her husband said many times with maddening repetition. '"Good would come of it – no harm could possibly come of it" – you have dinned this into my ears; now, perhaps, you will point out the good. I am taken away from my home and leave behind me a respectable family of which, I suppose, any father might be reasonably proud. I return to find the husband of my daughter lying drunk and incapable in the sight of my labourers –'

'Do I care if it was rhubarb wine or what it was? The man, a clergyman, a husband, a – a son-in-law – was *drunk!* I find my other girl standing calmly by, evidently pleased with the situation, while a young man – a man I always said we ought not to have into our house, a man with whom I will allow no infernal nonsense of love-making, as I have told you many and many a time – playing with her hair! Upstairs lies my dear little Bel – worth the lot of them lumped together – moaning in her pain, deserted by those who are not worthy to clean her dear little boots –'

'A nice, agreeable outcome of a week's tomfoolery! And how do we know where it's going to stop, eh? How do we know?'

When, later on, it became necessary to tell him of Tony Patten's engagement to appear before the Ornwich magistrates on Monday morning, his wrath knew no bounds.

In the privacy of the marital chamber he cursed by all his gods the rash young man who had shot old Pettifer's rabbits. He protested that while he remained in his house he would not speak a word to him, and he called upon his wife in forcible language to tell Tony to go – a task which Mrs Boyan naturally suggested that he should perform himself.

'Certainly!' the irate parent acquiesced. 'I'll tell him to go as soon as look at him.'

But he did not show the alacrity to carry the threat into execution which his zeal in the cause promised, contenting himself with treating the young man with scanty ceremony, according him a huffy silence when that was possible, or a hectoring style of conversation when compelled to address him.

Now, Bay having by this time also developed measles, Mrs Boyan passed most of her time in the children's bedroom, and had no thought for the young man under a cloud downstairs. Rica, too, remained in upper regions in attendance on the husband who, recovering from the effects of 'rhubarb wind,' was prostrate from a bad head and violent sickness, while Mary had not returned with her parents, but remained in London in readiness to join her hospital. It happened, therefore, that Tony Patten had no companion or help or defender in the unpleasant situation in which he found himself but Rosamond.

She was never a very judicious person, and she showed her resentment of Tony's treatment in a fiercely defiant attitude maintained towards her father, a method of procedure which did not help the young man at all.

'I've no quarrel with you, you know, Rosamond,' Mr Boyan told her more than once. His 'nut-brown maid' he had been wont to call her, and was proud of her straight, strong figure, and liked to pass his hand over the wealth of her red-brown hair. But now she pulled her head away petulantly from the hand that would have caressed it, refused the kiss he proffered, pouted in silence when, being sensible, she should have laughed and talked. While Tony was in disgrace her father found there was no conciliating Rosamond.

⋯⋎⟡⋏⋯

On the afternoon of the day following the return to Bunwick Hall, Tony Patten, cogitating with a very glum face as he smoked the pipe of meditation alone in the deserted tennis-court, found the situation was no longer tenable with honour, even with self-respect, and decided that he would put an end to it.

'I'll have it out with him and go,' Tony said.

And just then the master of the house appeared, walking with his quick, irritable step through the garden on his way to get his afternoon cup of tea, and Tony, giving himself no time for further reflection or repentance, walked up to him.

⋯⋎⟡⋏⋯

Rosamond, coming out ten minutes later to warn Tony that the tea was getting cold, stopped on her way to the tennis-court at the sound of her father's voice raised, as it always was, in anger.

'I repeat to you, you have not behaved as a gentleman,' the voice shouted. 'You have taken advantage of a position – a false position – in which the child should never have been placed.'

Rosamond could not see the speaker; a clipped hedge of sweetbriar separated her from the men. The instinct to run away, to be deaf to that which she was not intended to hear, was lamentably absent from Rosamond's composition. Her face grew paler, but she listened with all her ears.

'And I repeat,' said the other voice, which, although not so loud, was clearer and more incisive, and reached Rosamond's heart as easily as her ear, 'that I have done nothing of the kind – not by word or, so far as I know myself, by tone or look.'

Then the gusty voice of the father burst forth in an expletive which Rosamond jumped to hear.

'D—n it!' he cried. 'Didn't I catch you fooling with the girl's hair?'

121

He paused a minute there, but the statement was unfortunately irrefutable, and Tony was silent.

'Don't tell me!' roared the triumphant voice, then: 'Don't tell me! And don't let me hear a word more on this subject – ever – do you hear? Neither this year, nor next year, nor a hundred years hence. Not a word!'

A minute later Rosamond, creeping cautiously round the other side of the clipped hedge, found Tony standing motionless in the rose garden which the hedge protected, and saw her father stalking off, followed by the parlour-maid, who had presumably come out to fetch him, in the direction of the house.

'Tony,' said Rosamond, softly calling, 'come to tea.'

He lifted his eyes from the watch he held in his hand and looked at her with a dazed expression.

She joined him on the gravel walk which intersected the rose beds. 'Why are you looking so worried?' she asked him.

'I was thinking,' he told her. 'In the holidays, you know, I don't accustom myself to think. From want of use it becomes a painful process.'

'Is there any result?'

'The result is this: I've decided to walk the eight miles to Ornwich, put up at a hotel there for a couple of nights, and be in time for the magistrates' meeting on Monday morning. The word "rabbit" to your father is like a red rag to a bull, and it wouldn't be very pleasant to him for me to go to this accursed affair from his house.'

Rosamond's eyes filled with swift tears. 'Don't go, Tony,' she said. 'You know what my father's rages are. At any minute he may be as nice as nice to you again.'

He smiled at the wet eyes. 'Baby!' he said. 'I'm not afraid of your father's anger, my dear, but I owe it to him to relieve him of an unpleasant situation.'

He had returned his watch to his pocket, but pulled it out again. 'If I start now,' he said, 'I shall get a pleasant walk in the coolest part of the day. I'll go in and see Eustace and Rica and explain matters, and you'll say good-bye to your mother for me, Rosamond. Tell her that I will write, and that I thank her for everything.' Here he put out his hand. 'Good-bye, Rosamond,' he said.

But she would not take the hand, and she turned her face away from him, for she was crying.

Tony's hand dropped to his side. 'We've had a pleasant time,' he said. 'How long ago it seems already since we kept house together! Good-bye to the pleasant time. Good-bye, Rosamond.'

'I won't say good-bye,' said Rosamond, with a childish catching of the breath. 'I won't deliver any of your stupid messages. You can't leave – people's houses – without saying good-bye to – people. It's so frightfully ill-mannered! Come and see mother.'

She turned to lead the way to the house, but he stopped her with a touch upon her shoulder. 'There's just one word I want to say to you before I go. You were wrong about Mary. I always knew about the curate. Eustace told me – Rica had told him. With a married sister you can't expect to keep any family secrets, you see. I always knew – and you were quite wrong. Do you understand?'

Rosamond nodded her head, trying to blink the tears away, and gave utterance to a miserable, choking 'Yes.'

They stood silent for a minute or so, he waiting for her to recover herself, she waiting for something further from him.

'This is mother's part of the garden,' she presently said, offering the unnecessary information with apparent irrelevance. 'Roses are her favourite flower, did you know? That was why she named me Rosamond. When I was quite a little girl she gave this rose-bush – look! – my name to please me. Other people call it the Duke of Edinburgh, which is absurd. Mother and I call it the Rosamond. It's got only one flower, you see' – here, with her eager, shaking fingers, she detached it and held it out to him – 'only one, and it's for you.'

When they neared the open window of the library, in which room Rosamond had had the tea placed, there came to them the sound of strange voices.

'Visitors!' Tony said, and drew back. Rosamond, creeping cautiously forward, pressed her white-robed person against the creeper-grown wall, and, stretching her long neck, peeped into the room.

Instantly she flew back to Tony, gripped him by the collar of his coat, and dragged him out of sight.

'The Dodmans!' she whispered, with a wild chuckle across the sob which now and again rose in her throat, 'Mr and Mrs and Hetherington!'

Tony made up his mouth for a noiseless whistle. 'This is likely to be a lark,' he said.

'They've come to complain of the gooseberry-stealing – and other things. They're sitting three in a row facing the little window – you remember those dummies in the ventriloquist's entertainment? Just like it. Come round to the bay window and let's hear what they've got to say.'

It was Mr Boyan's voice, loud and assertive, which first struck upon the listeners' ears.

'I'm sorry you should have been inconvenienced, of course,' he said. 'Much obliged to you for letting me know. I'll speak to Dexter about it. There are some rather objectionable people, I know, at the Cherry-tree Cottages. The man is a poacher, and has been turned off. Assaulted your son, you say? Extraordinary proceeding!'

Hetherington raised his open hand and smacked his own cheek here noisily, and nodded at the master of the house, pulling his lips into a straight line across the face, and pursing them up into a pout again.

'It was the most unprovoked thing,' Mrs Dodman explained. 'My son has never set eyes on his assailant before or since – have you, my dear?' turning to Hetherington, who nearly shook his head off in the earnestness of his repudiation of any knowledge of Tony.

'The young woman, too, is a very forward young woman,' Mrs Dodman went on. 'I don't wish to complain of her manner to me, because I think I can make allowance for the poor young creatures of her class who know no better. But we strongly suspect her of having broken open our coach-house in order to liberate her sister – do we not, Hetherington?'

Hetherington blinked with his white-lashed lids and said, 'Strongly.'

'Ah! And what did you say her sister was doing in her coach-house?' Mr Boyan asked. His thoughts had evidently been otherwise; he had not listened altogether attentively to the details.

'She had been committing depredations,' the clergyman said. He was a withered, dark man, twenty years older than his wife, and, in spite of the heat of the day, he wore a short black cloak over his shoulders.

('Small and miserable-looking, and with a beak,' Rosamond said afterwards in describing him to her mother. 'Like a very old rook – with apologies to the rook.')

'Not the first of the female line who has fallen before the lusciousness of fruit,' Mr Dodman continued; he had an acquired deliberateness of enunciation which, in the reading-desk, drove his parishioners wild. 'She had designs upon my gooseberry bushes.'

'More than designs, dear,' his wife corrected. 'The gardener could almost swear that the boy who was her companion had eaten three. Hetherington,' she broke off to say in a warning undertone, 'it is not well-mannered to point, dear. What are you pointing at?'

Hetherington had turned suddenly round and descried the two listening faces at the bay window.

Being discovered, there was nothing for Rosamond and Tony to do but to advance into the room. The girl, very engaging-looking in her white dress, her beautiful hair loose about her back, bowed with a very stiff neck, and quite smilelessly, to Mrs Dodman, too much astonished to make any movement in response.

'It was poor little Bel, father,' Rosamond said, gaining his side, sure of his tenderness for the sick darling of his heart. 'She had often gathered dear old Mr Bryant's gooseberries and she went to get them again. This – lady – locked her in the coach-house and frightened her to death, and sent for the policeman, and, of course, I let her out, daddy.'

'My little Bel?' the father said. 'Locked up my little Bel?'

'Of course I let her out, daddy.' Here she turned and looked at Hetherington, who, with his mouth screwed up as if for a soundless whistle, was gazing with eyes of intensest admiration at Tony, in a suit of clean white flannels, still standing by the window. 'But I had to pay for it,' Rosamond said.

Mrs Dodman was very red in the face, and, for the moment, slightly flurried in manner. She had too good an opinion of herself, however, and was too sure of her own infallibility, to be seriously disconcerted. 'It seems to me there has been a mistake,' she said. 'I am bound to say, all the same, I don't hold myself responsible for the mistake. I naturally believed what this young lady led me to believe – that she was one of Mr Boyan's cottagers.'

'Instead of which I am one of Mr Boyan's daughters,' Rosamond said, and added, with a priggishness excusable, perhaps, under the circumstances, 'I fail to see that the fact should have made any difference.'

To Mrs Dodman it made a great difference. She proceeded with plausibility and a great flow of chatter to excuse herself, nay, even to laugh over the absurdity of her mistake. She had two quite distinct manners for her social superiors and for those who were of inferior station. Indeed, she was two quite different women. Rosamond decided that both manners were equally bad; she disliked either woman.

'This dear girl,' she said, with a heavy playfulness to her husband, 'was absolutely sweeping the cottage floor. Such a picture as she made! I remember thinking that all this beautiful hair was in the way. I think I even ventured to advise you to put it up. Such a sin as it would have been! I'm glad you did not take my advice –' and so on, striving to drown remembrance of her mistake in the shallow stream of her eloquence.

Hetherington had gone forward to Tony Patten standing apart from the group. He shook him energetically by the hand, and, still holding it, dragged him forward.

'This is the fellow that smacked my face,' he said to Mr Boyan. 'I didn't mind a bit. He's such a splendidly strong fellow. I say, you are a strong fellow, you know,' he said, and affectionately passed his claw-like red hand over Tony's sleeve. 'It stung, but I didn't mind. I like to see a fellow as strong as you.'

The visit could not be a very pleasant one, and was soon brought to a close.

'I'll see that you're no losers by the gooseberries. How many was it – three – my little girl had?' Mr Boyan said, stooping stiffly to sarcasm. He bowed a farewell to the Dodmans and did not see their out-stretched hands. He rang the bell sharply to have them shown to the door. 'I'm sorry you had the trouble of calling in a policeman,' he added. 'My poor little girl is ill in bed upstairs. Perhaps you will fetch the policeman to her there?'

Mrs Dodman took it all as a good joke and defended the position gallantly to the last.

They were barely out of the room before Mr Boyan turned to Tony. 'Slapped that little beggar's face, did you?' he asked, in new tones of approbation.

'Daddy,' cried Rosamond, interposing with kindling face, 'he made me kiss him – that little – reptile! And Tony –'

'Tony slapped his face,' her father said. He gave a laugh of satisfaction and put his hand on Tony's shoulder. 'I'd like to have been in your shoes for once, my boy,' he said.

'I'll bid you good-bye, sir,' Tony said. 'I'm off.'

'Good-bye?' echoed Mr Boyan. 'Nothing of the sort. What are you thinking about? I've got to see you through that affair before the magistrates. Have you forgotten? Stuff and nonsense about good-bye!'

Rosamond gazed with shining eyes upon the two men as they stood together, then flew from the room. The Dodmans' horse was being brought round, and the three of them – Mrs Dodman still defending her conduct with great volubility – were waiting on the step.

'A beautiful place and they seem delightful people. I'm very glad of this little misunderstanding which has given me the pleasure of knowing them,' Rosamond heard her say.

With her finger on her lip, the girl beckoned to Hetherington, who alone had seen her, and, obeying her gesture, he followed her into a room near the door.

126

'Look here! I don't believe you're a bad sort,' Rosamond said, 'and you've done Tony and me a good turn. And if you don't touch me with your hands, and don't do it more than once, and keep of the dimple, you may kiss me again if you like.'

Holding her body away from him, a precaution he remembered, she warily extended to him her round cheek of reddy-brown.

He looked at the cheek for a minute with his ferret eyes, his mouth working at a great rate, and then he shook his head.

'No, thank you,' Hetherington said. 'I think I'd better not. He's a fine fellow, but he hits so very hard, you know.'

⟿⤞⟐⤝⟾

The Reverend Eustace Patten is installed at East Wackham now. His parishioners are all agriculturists, and in them, at the present moment, he takes a deep interest. Being a good fellow as well as an enthusiast, he is liked and trusted by all classes, and manages the influence he possesses with a judiciousness said to be rare among his brethren of the cloth.

With the farmers he is always on the side of the men – the men 'patient of labour, with a little pleased' – pointing out to them how hard it is for the labourer to make two ends meet, how poorly he is fed, how few are his distractions, how closely he is shut away from the living world, how bare his existence is of opportunities of amusement, enlightenment, of cultivation. He is eloquent on the silent heroism displayed by a man who, year out year in, plods on in a hopeless round, slaving to drive starvation from his doors, to keep his wife and children covered, with no possible outlook but pauperdom in his enfeebled old age, at the end of it to die and leave a dead 'unprofitable name.'

For the intemperate he pleads too, reminding their judges what a temptation to the stomach, always craving the support the poor food will not give, is the pint o' beer over which too much of the labourer's wage goes; how easily, too, in an under-fed condition, the fumes of the adulterated beer, or even (as the reverend gentlemen never forgets to add) of the insidious home-made wine, will mount to and muddle the brain

To those who mark the signs of the times – and even in the out-of-the-world district subject to his ministry are a few who can project themselves beyond their personal, even parochial, affairs – he points to the growing scarcity of agricultural labourers as one of the questions with which the country will soon have to grapple. The time is fast coming, the clergyman thinks, when there will be none but the most inferior workmen – men who can get work in no other direction – who can be sent to labour in the vineyard. 'Look out for yourselves,' the Reverend Eustace says. 'You can't at the same time expect a blessing on your industry and grind the faces of the poor.'

To the men themselves their pastor preaches words of encouragement and patience.

'It seems hard, I grant you,' he says. 'And an outsider will not understand how a man, his wife and children, can live in decency on the wage you receive. It sounds impossible. But it can be done, I know,' says the Reverend Eustace, wrenching his jaw on one side and looking through his glasses with bright confidence in the men's faces. 'It can be done – for I've done it.'